A Little Too Fond of Cake

and other stories

Cecilia Peartree

This collection includes the title novella, A Little Too Fond of Cake, and a handful of short stories of various lengths and genres.

A Little Too Fond of Cake, a dark comedy of novella length (in 13 chapters), tells the separate but somehow inextricably connected stories of Claire and Jennifer, who both happen to be fond of cake, and of Claire's husband George's mysterious disappearance.

Contents

A Little Too Fond of Cake

Chapter 1 The Birthday Present
Chapter 2 Jennifer's Dream
Chapter 3 Claire's Vision
Chapter 4 Revenge is a Dish
Chapter 5 Claire Decides
Chapter 6 Jennifer's Plan
Chapter 7 In Trouble
Chapter 8 Attack
Chapter 9 Sanctuary
Chapter 10 Free Therapy
Chapter 11 DNA
Chapter 12 Seeing the Black Dog
Chapter 13 Detective Work

Deadly Embrace

In Search of a Saint (a Pitkirtly origin myth)

The Waiting Room

The Last Piece of the Puzzle 1

The Last Piece of the Puzzle 2

Locked Room

About the Author

A Little Too Fond of Cake

(a comedy of errors)

Chapter 1 The Birthday Present

The anticipation had been building all day, which was no doubt what George had planned. He waited until they were seated at the table in the restaurant to hand it over.

Claire looked at the pink envelope. 'Is this it?'

'Happy birthday!'

With a sudden premonition of doom, she opened the envelope very, very slowly, and slid out the folded piece of paper. It was decorated with balloons and unicorns and teddy bears, as if intended for a small girl of the kind that liked to wear pink or a princess outfit. Claire was wearing a plain dark blue tailored dress with a discreet silver pendant and matching bracelet. George had given her the jewellery in the good old days before they got married, while he was still trying to please her as opposed to improving her.

The balloons and so on couldn't conceal what else was on the paper. She flung it down on the table and scowled at him.

'Nutritional therapy sessions? Is this a joke? Where's my real birthday present?'

'Not so loud,' he hissed, belatedly adding, 'darling…. It was very expensive. Individual sessions come in at around a hundred pounds each.'

'So you got me a whole set because it was cheaper?'

'Sssh. Here comes the waiter.'

'Something to drink?' said the waiter, hovering a little way from the table. He was evidently afraid to approach them any closer.

'What shall we have, darling?' said George, turning his glower into a smile.

Turn your frown upside-down, thought Claire. Where on earth had that come from?

'I wouldn't mind a glass of house red, if that's all right,' she said.

'No champagne?' he asked, smiling.

She shook her head. This wasn't the moment for champagne, and if he couldn't see that…

He ordered a bottle of red. She didn't really care what label was on it. As far as she was concerned, the meal was already ruined.

As soon as the waiter had gone, he tried again.

'It's only because I'm concerned about your use of food to distract yourself from dealing with emotional issues,' he said in a tone that no doubt he imagined was a reasonable one, but which only inflamed her further.

'What emotional issues?'

Claire did try to keep her voice down this time. It wasn't her fault that it wobbled a little and, noticing this, she increased the volume to make up for it.

'That's exactly it!' he said, unfolding his napkin and arranging it on his lap with exaggerated precision. 'That's just what I mean. You don't even see them now, you're so good at distracting yourself.'

'It's your mother's fault, I suppose,' he said after a pause during which he seemed to expect her to say something, even if only in self-defence. 'She's always been one of these buttoned-up kind of women. I should've known…'

'What? You should've known what?'

'There's no need to shout – again. I mean, we should have had this out long ago. I'm kind of hoping the therapy will help you to find a way of expressing it.'

'It would be good if I knew what I was supposed to express,' she muttered.

He shook his head at her. 'You're over-thinking this. That's part of the problem.'

Somehow she got through the endless evening without even raising her voice again, not even when the waiter stumbled just behind her and sent a trickle of raspberry sorbet, just starting to melt, down the back of her dress. She tried to twist herself so that she could see what it looked like, but it was impossible, and she wasn't going to ask George to check for her. She didn't even want him to look at her again. He seemed to be seeing a completely different person from the one she saw every day in the mirror. A much larger person, for one thing. And one with an expression that was closed against any kind of emotion, for another. That definitely wasn't her.

'I'll take Bonzo out,' he said as soon as they got home.

Bonzo was a black woolly-looking dog, a designer dog that was part poodle and part Labrador. In the days when they'd still been speaking to each other – which now seemed a lifetime ago – they had speculated about which part was uppermost. He was a kind of middling sized dog, quite happy-go-lucky although with a strong aversion to men running. George had initially expected to be able to take the dog along when he went for a morning run, but he'd had to abandon the idea after only a couple of days. He said Bonzo obviously wasn't meant to be a runner's dog. Claire had tried running at one time and hated it, so she felt an irrational pleasure about the dog sharing her feelings on the subject, even although it meant she had to take on most of the walking.

It was a sign of George's displeasure, she knew, that he had voluntarily taken the dog out when that was officially her job. She just hoped he wouldn't abandon the animal somewhere along the way.

She got ready for bed, frowning at the sorbet residue on the back of her dress. Still, it would probably come out in the wash. And she couldn't blame George for it.

Unless he had bribed the waiter to pretend to stumble. She recalled the two of them holding a quiet conversation over by the dessert trolley. Which hadn't come anywhere near their table. He had ordered the sorbet for both of them without even asking what she wanted. Hmph! Anybody would think it was his birthday, not hers. He was welcome to the course of nutritional therapy sessions, too. After all, he was the one with an unhealthy relationship with food, constantly obsessing over it as he did.

It wasn't the first time he had decided she needed help, although the other times it had had nothing to do with food. Not long after they had first met, he had imagined she had an unhealthy relationship with alcohol and had talked her into going to group sessions to try and overcome the problem. In response, she had more or less given up drinking, at least when he was around to monitor her consumption. Anything rather than listen to these people droning on about their self-inflicted problems.

Soon after they got married, George had diagnosed her as having depression, on the flimsy grounds that she had left the washing-up lying in the sink after their first dinner-party. She had paid for private psychotherapy sessions, mostly to stop him grumbling, but after two of these she had decided the therapist was stringing her along to justify the hefty fee he charged, and she had gone straight home and ordered a dishwasher. Now she could stack the dishes inside it instead of leaving them in the sink. Mission accomplished.

Long after he and Bonzo were both asleep and snoring, these memories and other unhelpful thoughts raced frantically round in her head like rabbits on a greyhound track.

'First of all, full disclosure,' said the so-called nutritional therapist. 'I know what you're going through in terms of unhealthy eating. I've been there and done that myself. I'm so glad you've come to me. I look forward to working with you to overcome your hatred of your own body. Now tell me, what do you hope to achieve here?'

Claire's first reaction was to keep quiet. This approach had served her well during the other therapy sessions she'd been to. None of them had worked, needless to say. She hadn't come up the Clyde on a banana-boat. Nobody was going to make her change her ways.

'You can tell me anything,' said the therapist, smiling in a way that was probably supposed to set Claire at ease. 'I'm not easily shocked… What would you like to see when you look in the mirror in the morning?'

'A happy, smiling face?' said Claire, trying not to sound too sarcastic.

She couldn't remember when she had last seen herself smiling, especially first thing in the morning. She wasn't even human until she'd had her first cup of coffee. And a croissant, with butter imperfectly held in place by a layer of jam, or perhaps honey... Mmm, honey.

'There! You were smiling about something,' said the therapist woman with apparent satisfaction. 'Did you think of something nice? A lovely, sunny day out there, waiting for you to enjoy? A picnic with your other half?'

Claire suppressed a shudder. George hated picnics, and the last time she had talked him into one it had been particularly disastrous. A stranger's dog had rushed up, bitten Bonzo and run off with George's favourite rare roast beef and horse-radish sandwiches. Claire had felt bound to share her humble cheese and tomato roll with him, and then he had dropped half of his share in the sand and got up and marched back to the car, where he waited until she had collected up all the picnic equipment, put Bonzo on the lead and followed. Then Bonzo had turned out to have an injured ear which bled all over the interior of the car, and Claire had had to rush him to the vet later that day.

'He isn't keen on picnics,' she said now, hoping the therapist wouldn't ask any follow-up questions.

The therapist – what was her name again? Something to do with a river. Mrs Thamesford, or

11

was it Humberbridge? – only smiled again and seemed to be waiting for Claire to elaborate.

The smile had seemed a little false from the start, and now it was starting to be very annoying.

'He likes running,' said Claire. 'So it isn't that he never goes outside or anything.'

She didn't want Mrs Merseyferry to think George was some kind of vampire who lurked in dark corners, afraid to see daylight. Although he was fond of switching the light off when he was watching television, contrary to Claire's belief that viewing in the dark was bad for your eyes. Perhaps that had just been a childhood myth.

'Mmhm,' said the therapist. She coughed discreetly and shuffled her feet as if anxious to move. 'I'm afraid I have another client at half-past, so…'

Claire jumped up from the chair. 'Sorry – I must have lost track of time.'

The therapist had a diary on her lap suddenly. 'Shall we make another appointment for you, then?'

She looked unexpectedly eager. Claire discarded her half-formed plan to escape and never darken Mrs Severncrossing's door again. She might even have been able to ask for a partial refund if she had done so, and there were all kinds of things she might have spent it on – all kinds of cake, that was. There was a really special bakery at the corner of this very street. Still, she didn't have the heart to disappoint the woman. This was probably her only source of income, after all.

She made another appointment for the following week. This way George wouldn't be able to say she hadn't tried.

Chapter 2 Jennifer's Dream

Jennifer Avonbridge was about to drown in pancake mix. She tried all the different strokes she had learnt during her swimming phase a few years back, apart from butterfly, which she had never quite got to grips with. The instructor had tried every trick in the book to help her master it, and it still rankled that she'd been unable to forge forward, both arms out, sending tidal waves out in front of her as some of the others did. Only their tidal waves wouldn't have been quite as violent as hers. In fact, her friend Yvonne, who had been persuaded to come along to the classes with her, barely made a ripple when she launched herself on the water. But then, Yvonne had never had a problem with weight gain. She was one of these people who could eat what they liked.

In theory, Jennifer should hate Yvonne. In practice, the woman had been her best friend for more years than either of them liked to recall.

She reached the side of the giant mixing-bowl and clung on to the rim, gasping. She peered over the edge at the table top, gazing with longing at the pot of cream and the tin of golden syrup that sat there, waiting to decorate the pancakes. Oh yes, and there was a banana too. Always the healthy option.

Jennifer woke up with a start and found herself clinging to the edge of the bedside table with both hands. Her legs were entangled in the duvet and it took her several minutes to extricate herself.

Pancake mix, of all things! She shuddered.

Friday was her fast day, so she sipped at her cup of hot water with lemon juice, trying to tell herself that would be enough to see her through the morning's therapy sessions. And after all, she wouldn't have any credibility as a nutritional therapist if she let herself revert to looking like a great fat white slug. Were slugs even white? Weren't they a kind of slimy grey colour? That certainly wouldn't be a good look.

She glanced at her diary and groaned. Claire Harper. Her husband had paid for the course of therapy, and Jennifer had a feeling Claire wasn't entirely on board with the idea, to say the least. Was this the latest battle in a long-running marital dispute? She would have preferred not to get involved in anything like that, having been a casualty herself in the past. Let them slog it out for themselves without dragging in any outsiders. She didn't want to become collateral damage, and she particularly didn't want her therapy business to suffer in any way. Hard enough to keep it up and running as it was, what with rising rents and ever-increasing utility bills for the tenement flat just off the Royal Mile that she lived and worked in.

The consulting room wasn't even anything to write home about, she reflected as she waited for Claire later that morning, trying to ignore the hunger pangs. Normally she'd be looking forward to lunch about now, if you could call it lunch. Today she would just be boiling the kettle and slicing yet another lemon.

Claire sat back in the chair. Jennifer could see she wasn't actually all that overweight. Just a few extra pounds here and there. But the husband was right to intervene if he thought her eating was a problem, and anyway, Jennifer's livelihood depending on convincing people they should take control of their appetites and their lives as opposed to letting everything get out of hand and then trying to pick up the pieces.

'You've come back, then,' she said now. 'This is a really important step you've taken.'

Claire looked vaguely surprised.

'I haven't actually done anything yet,' she said. 'I mean, about the eating thing. I had two red velvet cupcakes, one after the other, when I got home the last time. I had to hide the packet from George. He wouldn't have understood.'

Jennifer tried not to wince.

'But you've remembered it and admitted it to me,' she said. 'And you must have felt some kind of shame, if you hid the packet.'

Claire appeared to consider this for a moment, then shrugged. 'I suppose. But it's more of an instinctive reaction now. To hide things from him. He just tends to over-react, and I didn't have the energy for it.'

Tell me about it, thought Jennifer grimly, wondering again why she had booked Claire

Harper in today knowing it was one of her fast days. She hardly had the energy to keep the encouraging smile on her face.

'It's possible your energy levels had dipped after the sugar rush from the cupcakes,' she said.

'For real?' said Claire.

Jennifer nodded. 'That's part of the problem.'

Claire was quiet for a moment, and then asked, 'I don't suppose you have a can of juice anywhere about, do you, Mrs Ironbridge?' She glanced round the room, possibly looking for a drinks fridge. 'I could really do with a Coke right now. It's all this talking, I think.'

'We haven't really done much talking yet,' said Jennifer. 'Or maybe you're not used to expressing your thoughts and feelings.'

Claire made a face. 'No, not really.'

'You really can say anything to me, you know. That's what I'm here for. And by the way, do call me Jennifer.'

Claire glanced round the room again, this time with the appearance of a wild animal caught in a trap. She suddenly got to her feet. 'I've got to go now, Mrs Tyneford. Thank you.'

Before Jennifer could stop her, either by physically getting between her and the door or by coming out with soothing words to ease her panic, Claire darted away. Jennifer sat and listened to the sound of her feet on the stone stairs, and to the bang of the front door once she reached ground level.

A panic attack, obviously. Jennifer had never before thought of herself as in any way threatening, but she was also no stranger to irrational anxieties and, having already worked out that Claire's eating problem had very little to do with actual eating, so she wasn't entirely amazed by this hasty exit.

Would Claire ever come back? Wait and see, Jennifer told herself. Be patient. Be here for her if she does return.

Meanwhile, she had better get the kettle on and slice the next lemon. She didn't want to end up dehydrated as well as extremely hungry. The mention of red velvet cupcakes hadn't helped at all. She could almost picture them now. They'd probably have a half-inch layer of icing – maybe nearer an inch - with a dusting of chocolate on top. And chocolate sauce in the middle, but not so much of it that it squooshed out all over everything.

Enough!

She heaved herself out of the chair, steadfastly ignoring the black spots that tended to appear before her eyes intermittently on fast days, switched the kettle on and fetched the lemon out of her bag. As she waited for the water to boil, she told herself firmly that she didn't feel faint, that fast days weren't going to do her any harm and that it was all worthwhile in any case.

If she said it to herself often enough, she might even start to believe it.

Chapter 3 Claire's Vision

Claire eyed the therapist uneasily. The woman looked even more like a bird of prey than before with her thin, narrow face and sharp nose. Had she been eating at all? Maybe she couldn't afford to eat. Claire considered directing her to the nearest food bank at the end of the session. Nutritional therapy might not pay very well, although George had said it was very expensive and she must complete the course. But then the rent on this posh flat would be extortionate, despite the stone staircase and the bicycle you could only just squeeze past when you came in at the front door. Then there was the heating. Did the old stone walls retain heat, or just cold? It wasn't all that warm in the room.

'Thank you for coming back today,' said Mrs Tyneford. Claire still wasn't sure she'd got the right name, but the woman hadn't complained when she'd used it the last time.

'I wasn't going to,' said Claire. 'But then George reminded me about the cost, and said, well, I'd better not tell you what he said…'

She shut up then. Mrs Tyneford didn't need to know about the squabble they'd had, or about George's not very well-veiled threat to walk out on her if she didn't pull herself together and get on with it. In a way she wished he would just go. Then at least she'd know where she was and she could decide for herself how many cupcakes she deserved that day, among other things.

'You can tell me about it if you think it would help,' said the therapist.

She almost sounded as if she didn't care what Claire said. Maybe it was time to try something new.

Claire cleared her throat. She could really do with a Cola right now, the full-fat kind, straight from the fridge. She glanced around the room to see if a fridge had magically appeared since the last time. Surely the therapist's throat must get dry with all the talking she had to do in the average day.

Before Claire could speak, Mrs Tynebridge continued in what seemed to be intended as an encouraging tone, 'It's all right. Really. You can say anything here. I won't judge you.'

'I remember my mum won a prize at a cake show once,' Claire told her. 'It was for a Victoria sponge with cream and strawberry jam in the middle, spread so thickly that they oozed out when you bit into it. There was just enough icing sugar on the top too. I remember the cream ran all down my front when we divided it up afterwards, but she didn't mind, just laughed and wiped it off my frock with a bit of kitchen roll.'

The therapist looked as if she might speak again, but Claire carried on regardless.

'Of course, you don't get people baking their own cakes so much those days, because there's so much of it in the shops. There's a place just round the corner where you can get those French style macarons, all different colours. They sometimes have the deep purple ones. You don't even have to bite into them – they just melt in your mouth. But then I think that used to be a slogan for some chocolate brand too. Don't wait until they melt in your hand. I didn't really mind if they melted in my hand, though. You could always just lick the melted chocolate off your fingers. It tasted the same either way.'

Again Mrs Tynebridge seemed as if she wanted to speak, but Claire was on a roll by then – probably a bacon roll with lots of tomato ketchup – and held up a hand to forestall the interruption.

'The same with those jam doughnuts – if you bite into them in the wrong place, the jam oozes out on to your hand, or down your front if you're not careful. If I get some on my top, I just scrape it off and put it back on the doughnut, and of course if it's on my fingers I lick it off. Mmm. I can almost taste it now… And the same with chips, I find.'

'Chips - with jam?' said the therapist faintly.

Claire's words rolled on.

'The best way to eat them is straight from the bag, with your fingers, licking off the salt and vinegar and the oil they're cooked in, as you go along. Maybe there's a deep-fried Mars Bar for afters, if you're lucky. Or an ice-cream, if the shop sells them as well. You know how I like my ice-cream?'

'No,' said the therapist.

She was sitting back in the chair staring at Claire with a look of desperate hunger in her eyes.

'In one restaurant I've been to, you can get a dish with lemon sorbet, proper ice-cream, tiny wee meringues and chocolate or toffee sauce poured over the top of everything. And one of those posh wafers that really taste of something. The trouble is, I usually fancy a little something else to eat on the way home from there, so I sometimes call in at the fish and chip shop after, for a battered sausage or two... Sorry – are you a vegetarian?'

'I don't think there's anything more I can do for you,' said Mrs Tynebridge, returning with a snap from whatever faraway fast-food paradise she had been transported to by Claire's words. 'I believe you should seek a different kind of help in future.'

Claire smiled and said goodbye.

If she hadn't hovered in the entrance to a close not far from the front door, she wouldn't have seen Mrs Tynebridge sneak into the baker's shop just along the road and come out with a cake-box, and neither would she have seen the woman sidling into the sweetie shop beyond that and emerging with the biggest chocolate bar in the world sticking out of the top of her handbag.

All that self-denial must have been really bad for her. Claire was glad to have been able to do something about it.

Chapter 4 Revenge is a Dish

It was all Claire Harper's fault.

Jennifer surveyed the disaster area that was her kitchen table. It was just about sagging in the middle under the weight of cakes, doughnuts, macarons and chocolate bars. She didn't know how she had even fitted them all into her shopping bags or carried them up the stairs to her flat for that matter.

The worst thing about it was that most of the goodies on display now bore the signs that someone had taken at least a couple of bites out of each of them, and in several cases a good deal more than that, judging by the scattering of crumbs that decorated the table in between cakes. She knew who that someone was. So much for the career as a nutritional therapist, which she had been so optimistic about. If only that woman hadn't come into her consulting room...

Who did Claire Harper think she was? Jennifer's anger started to build up, just as the nausea resulting from an overdose of sugar and fat wore off. There had been no point in Claire even thinking about therapy until she had faced up to her eating problem and decided she was ready to do something about it. She had displayed all the signs of a woman who was quite content to eat herself to death and enjoy it. No remorse about what she must have put her family through, no fear of all the illnesses she could potentially be in line for… Why should anyone in the medical profession – Jennifer counted herself in that number – even bother with her?

Jennifer moaned aloud, imagining herself facing her colleagues at the Association of Food Therapists' annual conference, at which she was due to give a talk about how she had converted an unhealthy love affair with food into an abiding love for wellness? If they ever found out about this episode, her reputation would be in ruins.

It was Claire's fault, but it was up to Jennifer to do something about it before the woman drove yet another medical practitioner out of their chosen career. Anger was a dish best served cold – or was that revenge? And why did she have to think of dishes at that moment?

Ideally she should sweep what was left of the cakes into the bin, but some residual memory of childhood hunger stopped her from doing it. Maybe if she only ate one cake a day until they were all gone… Maybe if she invited her friend Yvonne round for a tea party to celebrate something or other. Neither of them would have a birthday for months yet. There was the royal Jubilee, of course, though she wasn't particularly a royalist and she guessed Yvonne wasn't either. Still, Yvonne could probably eat most of the cakes without having to worry about putting on any weight. It was worth thinking about.

The other option, of course, was to force-feed them to Claire Harper the next time she came here for a session. If she ever came back. Surely the shame of having divulged her lurid cake fantasies would stop her?

It wasn't until she had a wakeful spell in the middle of the night that Jennifer began to wonder about George Harper, who after all had been the one to sign his wife up for nutritional therapy sessions in the first place. What did he think of his wife's non-existent progress to date? Had she even confided her doubts about the therapy to him?

Almost as if she had conjured him up by thinking of him, he called the following morning, His tone was peremptory, almost accusing.

'Claire isn't making any progress. Is your operation a scam? I understood you were fully qualified and experienced as a therapist.'

'I do need a certain amount of buy-in from the client for this to work,' said Jennifer coolly.

'Buy-in? Are you suggesting this is Claire's fault?'

'Not necessarily. But it might have been a good idea to discuss the idea with her, instead of springing it on her as a surprise.'

'It was a birthday present, for God's sake! It was meant to be a surprise!'

'Yes, but...'

'Are you trying to put the blame on me now? I don't believe this!'

He seemed to be deliberately working up his indignation. She thought he would likely ask for a refund any minute, but it was worse than that.

'Do you have a professional body I can complain to? This is completely unacceptable.'

'I'm sorry, but…'

'Never mind sorry. I'll make you sorry.'

'Therapies can take longer than you imagine to have a noticeable effect,' she said, but he ended the call before she even reached the end of the sentence.

A pity, because she could have warned him not to expect instant results or even to hope for them. A longer-term change of life style would be far more effective in almost every case. Still, she guessed from the tone of their conversation that he wasn't prepared to put up with any significant delay before seeing results. Maybe he envisaged his wife as being transformed by losing a few pounds in weight into the kind of wife he would be proud to be seen in public with. The kind of wife other men envied him for having. Somebody who would boost his masculine ego.

Hmph!

Jennifer slumped into the nearest chair and, operating on auto-pilot, reached for the nearest cake-tin, opened it and grabbed a cake at random. It was halfway to her mouth before she stopped herself.

It won't do any good to start eating unhealthily again, she told herself firmly.

But just a couple of bites won't hurt, surely?

She flung the cake away from her and slammed down the lid of the cake tin. She should have thrown it all in the bin, and never mind the waste of food. Then she would have been hungry until she saw Claire Harper again – hungry for cake, and hungry for revenge.

She deliberately reduced her calorie intake for the rest of the week to make sure of this.

The evening before Claire's next appointment, as Jennifer contemplated the plate that was almost completely covered with various salad leaves, the solid mass of green only enlivened a little by the presence of a couple of small tomatoes, the phone rang.

'It's Claire Harper here,' said a small voice.

Of course it was. And Jennifer knew exactly what the woman was going to say.

'You aren't coming back, are you?' she asked.

'No.' Still the small voice. 'I just don't think it's doing either of us any good.'

'Don't worry about me,' Jennifer heard herself saying, slightly to her own surprise. 'Give yourself another chance. Maybe you can still turn things round.'

'I don't think so.'

What was that catch in Claire's voice? Was it a suppressed sob?

Don't start feeling sorry for her, Jennifer told herself, although she suspected it was too late. Claire had brought it all on herself. She should have stood up for herself against that nasty husband of hers and told him where to shove his so-called birthday present. It had to be her own decision to mend her ways, not his.

She opened her mouth to say something along these lines and closed it again without speaking.

'I'm sorry,' said Claire. 'But I just wondered if you could maybe refund some of the money? Only I've seen a really nice bag online that I want to buy, and I thought...'

Jennifer could hardly believe her ears. So Claire thought some retail therapy would work better than the face-to-face professional kind, did she? The woman badly needed help, for all sorts of reasons.

'I'd have to pay it back into Mr Harper's account,' she said coolly. 'He was the one who paid for the course of treatment, after all.'

'Treatment? Is that what you call it?' said Claire.

Jennifer took a deep breath before replying. She didn't want Claire bad-mouthing her to all her friends – if she had any friends, which was extremely doubtful.

'I'm affiliated to the Association of Food Therapists,' she said. 'We're a professional organisation. We offer various courses of therapeutic treatment. You can look up our website. It's possible that one of my colleagues can offer you something more suited to your needs.'

There was silence, and Jennifer realised that Claire had ended the call, either during her formal speech or immediately after it.

She hadn't been able to bring herself to throw out all the cakes left over from her silly splurge of the previous week but had put some away in tins and placed them on top of the tallest cupboard in the kitchen, from where she would have to stand on a chair to retrieve them. She knew they were still fit to eat – the best-before dates alone had shown her how many of the ingredients were artificial.

Moving stiffly as if on auto-pilot, she stood up and dragged the chair over to the cupboards. She climbed on it and reached up for the first tin.

Chapter 5 Claire Decides

It took Claire a while to decide what to do about the therapy sessions and the money. She could pretend to George that she was still going to see Mrs Call-Me-Jennifer Thamesford – what was the woman's last name anyway? – and go off and do something else instead, which was tempting. It would be like skiving off school. She could do whatever she liked with the time, within reason – have afternoon tea in two different tea-rooms, one after the other, meet her mother, whom she hardly ever saw because George didn't like her, go to the pictures and see something that George would have called 'fluffy', his word for any form of culture he disapproved of, from chick-lit to television crafting contests.

As she was walking across the Meadows in the middle of the afternoon when she had been due to go to the next therapy session but was actually on the way to her first choice of tea-room, she experienced a sudden flash of insight.

At first she thought she might have been struck by lightning, for dark clouds had loomed over her oppressively as she closed the garden gate, there had been a distant rumble that might have been thunder if it hadn't been traffic, and she had wondered whether she was utterly reckless to have come out of the house without a proper raincoat, but she was still on her feet and not lying in an untidy heap on the ground, so it couldn't have been that.

Her feet, though, had come to a complete standstill, and people were giving her funny looks as they passed her on the path.

Was this to be the pattern for the rest of her life?

The next flash of insight came quickly after this one and was even more unexpected.

Why was she still with George anyway?

She dug her phone out of her bag and called her mother. This was the kind of moment when, in theory at least, every woman needed her mother. In this case her older sister Marilyn might have been of more help, only she lived in Barcelona while Mum was closer to hand and could reasonably be expected to rush to Claire's side in this time of crisis.

'Does it have to be today? Only I've got my crafting group this afternoon, and I was hoping to get a wee bit of time to myself to practise my quilling before then.'

'Quilling?'

'It's a thing with paper. We were all supposed to do it for homework, but I haven't had time.'

'Homework?' Claire tried to stop her voice rising to a disbelieving wail. 'What do you need to do homework for? I thought you went to your crafting group for fun.'

'It is fun,' said her mother. 'But you only get out what you put in. Some of the others have been to evening classes,' she added darkly. 'Jean Robertson's always getting ahead of herself with the papercraft.'

'Oh, dear, we can't have that!' said Claire, and ended the call.

What was the use of living within reach of your mother if she wouldn't lift a finger to help in an emergency? Hadn't Mum realised how serious this was?

Claire sent a quick text to Marilyn just to ask whether she planned to come over to Edinburgh any time soon. If not, she supposed they'd have to do a video-call instead, which wasn't quite the same. She knew Marilyn wouldn't get the full picture of what was happening to her little sister unless they were in the same room together. She realised she hadn't wanted to press Marilyn to come over because her sister and George never seemed comfortable in the same room. Their conversation, if they were forced to do it, was stilted and they tried not to look at each other.

She was already in the tea-room when she received a short and unsatisfactory reply from Marilyn. Apparently there was some kind of a crisis in Barcelona too, and Marilyn didn't even have time for a video-call. Her crisis couldn't be as bad as Claire's, though. Marilyn had taken the precaution of discarding her husband some time ago.

She recklessly ordered afternoon tea for two, telling the waitress she was expecting a friend to join her. Maybe nobody would notice the friend's failure to appear, but she could always say there had been some unforeseen delay caused by an accident, a road closure, the cancellation of a train, sudden illness – really, the possibilities were endless. It was almost too easy to think up excuses. Maybe she should give up her job and take up creative writing.

Later, fuelled by carbohydrates, she walked back across the Meadows. She had taken a decision. Either she would have to go or George would. She quite liked the idea of throwing all his belongings into a heap in the front garden and having the locks changed while he was still at work. She could almost see the expression of total disbelief on his face, and hear him hammering on the front door begging to be let back in. She hoped he wouldn't hammer hard enough to break the glass.

Was there time to get hold of a locksmith that day?

As she let herself into the flat, Claire thought that she should probably be grateful to Mrs Forthbridge, and maybe even indirectly to George himself, for getting her out of her comfort zone and unintentionally encouraging her to see her life in a new light. Because she was fairly sure

Jennifer Ironbridge wouldn't have put up with George for half as long as she had. Marilyn wouldn't have either.

At least they didn't have children who might be upset when they separated. Claire thought she would have felt duty bound to stay a bit longer if other lives would be affected.

In her mind she and George were already living apart. She glanced round the front room, imagining how it would look when she got rid of the stark masculine décor and imported some of her mother's patchwork cushions and maybe a display cabinet for the collection of cat ornaments that currently languished in a drawer in the spare bedroom.

The dog barked to let her know he'd had enough of being shut in the kitchen. Claire sighed. She half-hoped George might take the dog with him when he left, but on the other hand, she'd been the one who wanted what he'd called a designer dog in the first place, and she was afraid if she forced the issue George might abandon the animal on the doorstep of the cat and dog home.

This in turn made her feel guilty in advance for the fate she had imagined for Bonzo as a result of the split-up, and she decided to take him out for an overdue walk, which would use up some of the many calories she'd just ingested and might take her mind off how she was going to break the news to George.

During the walk she decided it wasn't exactly a case of breaking the news. Giving him an ultimatum? That wasn't it either, because she knew there was nothing he could do that would make a difference, even if she allowed him a month, or six months, or six years to change his ways. He would still be the same irritable, censorious, controlling person he'd always been.

She would just have to tell him she couldn't live with him any longer, Claire decided as she and Bonzo, feet dragging, left Holyrood Park and walked the hard streets that would take them home.

After psyching herself up as much as possible on the way, then switching on the oven and getting something out of the freezer for dinner, she was disappointed when George didn't arrive home at the expected time. But then, he worked on the fringes of the city and the buses were always likely to get stuck in a traffic jam, especially with all the road works that were currently in progress. And the service wasn't all that frequent, so if one bus was cancelled he might have had to wait anything up to forty minutes for the next.

It was a bit annoying having to postpone her big announcement. She was afraid of having second thoughts if she left it too long.

Another hour went by. She switched off the oven and made herself a sandwich. When George came home, he could do the same. He might at least have called to let her know he'd be late.

Wait a minute – it wasn't his badminton night, was it? Claire frowned. She could have sworn it was Thursday, and badminton was usually on Tuesdays. Unless he was playing in some kind of special event – that wouldn't have been unheard-of. She looked in the umbrella-stand in the front hall, where he kept his badminton racquet. It was still there, along with the one she had used a couple of times and then abandoned when she realised she had a phobia about shuttlecocks. Was there a word for that?

She opened the front door as if expecting him to be walking down the path towards her. There wasn't even anybody on the street outside. They must all be indoors watching one of those interminable talent shows. The one with cakes, which she studiously avoided, or the ice-skating one, which gave her flashbacks to her own failed attempts at ice-skating, years back.

Another hour passed, and another, and there was still no sign of George. Claire wasn't exactly worried, or at least she told herself she wasn't, but she would have preferred to know when he'd be back. What if she locked the front door and went to bed, and he had forgotten his key and couldn't get in? What if he hammered on the door and woke the neighbours?

He must have his phone with him, though. He could have called by now. This was just pure selfishness.

She let Bonzo out in the back garden, which was part of his bedtime routine. He snuffled around a bit and disturbed something in the undergrowth at the far end, which she'd been hoping George and Frank from the first-floor flat would tidy up soon between them. If that was a mouse… or a rat.

'Bonzo!' she called, but quietly.

She didn't want the dog to catch some hideous disease from any vermin that happened to have set up home among the fallen leaves and creeping ivy. Surely he wouldn't go after a squirrel, would he? She didn't think labradoodles were supposed to be ferocious hunters.

He came to her side and gazed up at her longingly. Oh, yes. Treat time.

At least she could lock the back door securely behind him, and it would be silly to go to bed leaving the front door unlocked. George would just have to call if he found himself locked out. It was past time for him to call anyway. So inconsiderate of him not to!

She lay awake for some time. It was typical of George not to turn up when she had something specific to say to him. Almost as if he had guessed it was going to be something unpleasant. Although he was often abrupt and dismissive when speaking to her, she knew he expected her just to accept this as part of the price of being married to him.

The price she was no longer prepared to pay.

Chapter 6 Jennifer's Plan

Jennifer had to cancel several therapy sessions the following week, because she wasn't in the right place mentally to listen to anybody's eating issues. She hadn't got through all the cakes and had even thrown one or two away, but that only meant she was tempted to replenish her supply every time she walked past the bakery on the corner. She couldn't in all conscience help anybody else if she couldn't even help herself. She didn't like to think about the effect of all this on her income either.

Claire Harper didn't know what she had done.

But she would find out, Jennifer vowed. It was time to make a plan.

This was when she unearthed the project management tool she had found useful when setting up the nutrition business only six months before. It had been languishing on the computer, unwanted, unloved…

She pushed these unhelpful images to one side. There was no way she would think of a piece of software as a personification of herself. Instead she would harness its full capabilities to plot the downfall of her enemy. She stabbed at the keyboard, imagining a dagger in one hand while movements of the mouse swept the cursor across the screen, as deadly as a sabre. Was there a way of actually turning the cursor into a sabre? Maybe if you were a teenager playing games, she thought dismissively. But this wasn't a game.

What did she know about Claire Harper? Apart from the fact that the woman was a danger to everybody around her and was married to a man who spoke in a peremptory tone and had a particularly unsympathetic manner. Well, she had the woman's address and phone number. Maybe Claire had a social media presence from which Jennifer could deduce a bit more.

Jennifer didn't believe in having personal social media accounts. She tried to keep them on a purely professional level, re-posting articles about problematic relationships with food, or recipes for healthier eating, all without giving away too much about herself. She soon discovered – surprise, surprise! – that Claire was not at all like her in this respect. There were random, informal pictures of her with her husband, who almost always seemed to be frowning, and with her family and friends – and there was a dog!

She sensed at once that the dog could be the key to this whole operation. The dog would need to be walked, maybe several times a day, and Claire's attention would surely be too taken up with the dog when they were out for her to notice somebody following her.

Stalking her…

Another thought to be pushed to the back of her mind, because what she was planning to do was surveillance. She would carry out surveillance with the quite reasonable objective of – what? What was she going to do to Claire? Would she ever actually attack the woman, or would that happen only in her imagination? Maybe her aim was merely to back Claire into a corner, even metaphorically speaking, and to explain to her that she had ruined Jennifer's business and set back her recovery from cake addiction by months, if not years.

And then the other woman would weep remorsefully and promise to mend her ways, return to therapy and recommend Jennifer to all her friends. After all, Claire must have friends or even family who would benefit from eating more healthily. Everybody had friends who were that bit too fond of a nice afternoon tea with these tiny sandwiches and vegan sausage rolls on one layer of the cake stand, macarons and strawberry tarts on the next, little fondant fancies nestling close to miniature slices of Victoria sponge on the top level…

Stop it! Jennifer told herself. You know this isn't helping.

She briefly considered the possibility of acquiring a dog of her own, to give her a watertight excuse to use the same places to walk it as Claire used for hers. She could even go there in disguise and strike up a conversation with Claire. They might become friends – and only then would she move in for the kill. Her dog would be larger and fiercer than Claire's dog, which was one of these designer breeds. Maybe she could get hold of a huskie, for instance. She was sure they could hold their own in a fight with some kind of poodle crossbreed.

For the second time in five minutes Jennifer had to tell herself to stop it. It was no use. It would take ages to get a dog – she knew her friend Yvonne hadn't been able to find one for months, because she too lived in a tenement flat and the dog rescue people wouldn't let her have the one she wanted. Yvonne had ended up moving to the Stockbridge colonies just so that she could get a dog.

Jennifer had no intention of disrupting her life further by moving to Stockbridge, and even if she did, she knew she didn't really want to own a dog. The effort involved was relentless. It was worse than having children. Not that she knew anything about children, and probably never would. She would just have to be more subtle. Maybe take up running – that would give her a reason to be out first thing in the morning, last thing at night or any time in between that turned out to be Claire's dog-walking time.

She discounted the idea that George might do any of the walking. On Claire's social media pages, the dog was never pictured with him. There was very little chance, therefore, of bumping into him during her surveillance operation. She had little doubt that he would call the police immediately if she suspected her of anything that resembled stalking.

There was that word again. No, she wouldn't even think about it. That word didn't feature in her mental dictionary at all. Or in her personal thesaurus.

She would have to get up earlier than usual, of course, if she wanted to catch Claire and the dog. Presumably the woman walked her dog before going to work. Where did she work again? Had she even said?

Jennifer got up from her swivel chair, the slight stiffness in her knees reminding her she had been sitting for too long, and went through to the other room, her consulting-room, to fish out Claire's file from the filing cabinet. Even with computer booking systems and everything, she still kept manual files on all her clients. She was terrified of losing all the information to hackers and scammers. Her hand-written notes were worth their weight in gold.

How much did they in fact weigh? she mused as she leafed through Claire's file, which was of course fairly lightweight compared to one or two of the rest. Probably not enough to support her through this tricky patch, even if they could somehow be magicked into gold.

Chapter 7 In Trouble

George still hadn't come home. At times Claire wondered whether to call the police and report him missing, but she had the feeling he'd gone off in a huff and would just as suddenly reappear. He would have hated to have the police out looking for him.

He hadn't been at work either. A man from the HR department at his workplace – one of the financial companies at Edinburgh Park – had called on the Monday after he had first failed to arrive home, asking why he hadn't come into work and expressing the hope, which for some reason sounded like a threat, that he hadn't been taken ill over the weekend. Claire had lied and said he'd been called away urgently to his mother's deathbed. She fervently hoped George's mother would never find out about this deception. As far as she knew, for they weren't close, the woman practically lived on the golf course and was fitter than anybody else Claire knew.

But what if George's mother was struck by lightning at the eighteenth hole and the lie turned out to be true after all?

Come on, Claire, she told herself, how likely is that? She was tempted to Google how many golfers were struck by lightning in the average year, but that would definitely be tempting fate.

On Wednesday the man from HR called again. Claire was at work herself by then. She worked at a desk in the back bedroom, from which she sent out social media content all round the world on behalf of several smallish companies. George didn't think of it as a proper job at all, of course, but her income had made it possible for them to buy the flat and live in it in reasonable comfort, and to support an expensive designer dog like Bonzo.

The dog jumped up when he heard the ringtone, and began running round in circles, sending a coffee-cup and a pile of magazines flying.

She sighed as she answered the call.

'Mrs Harper?' said the HR man, one of the people she least wished to hear from. 'Greg Lawson here. Just checking in with you again. Have you heard from George yet?'

'I'm afraid he's still with his mother,' said Claire hastily, grabbing Bonzo's collar on one of his circuits of the room.

'Oh, dear,' said Greg Lawson. 'Difficult for him, I know, but could you possibly ask him to call us? We have something we'd like him to glance over before we finalise it... I haven't been able to get an answer on his mobile. But I appreciate that he may have switched it off altogether, in the circumstances.'

The word 'circumstances' was pronounced in a macabre undertone. Or maybe it was just Claire who found it macabre. The call had put her even more on edge than she had been for days.

'Yes, I believe he probably has,' she said as calmly as she could. 'I don't think anybody would want to die to the sound of ringtones.'

There was a pause.

'Of course not,' he said. 'If you have any other way of getting in touch with George, please do so as soon as possible.'

The call ended.

Claire held her phone in her hands for several moments, debating with herself whether to try sending her husband a direct message. She had been holding back from calling because she really didn't want to speak to him, but she knew she couldn't keep his employers at bay for ever. Sending him a message would be easier than calling. In any case, if he'd really switched his phone off or even lost it or damaged it, she wouldn't get through, whereas he might have access to a computer or other device and he'd be able to retrieve a message that way.

It took her ages to compose a suitable message. Honestly Claire, she said to herself, nobody would think you worked in social media.

She wasn't entirely satisfied with the message but in the end she just sent it anyway. She didn't say anything about being worried about him, just that he should get in touch with work as soon as he could. She had almost forgotten that his mother's deathbed was a lie and had to stop herself from mentioning it.

There was no immediate reply, of course. But then he might only have contacted work without bothering to reply to her. It was odd, though. She hadn't realised until that moment how displeased he was with her. Maybe he'd seen the eating therapy as some kind of test, or as a last throw of the dice before he gave up on her altogether.

It was typical of George to infuriate her even more by walking out on her before she could walk out on him. Not that she would actually have walked out. She had put too much effort into this flat to give it up easily. She had put a bit of effort into George too, but sometimes you just had to cut your losses.

The next morning there was Greg Lawson again at the other end of the line.

'We were wondering if you'd managed to get in touch with George?' he asked. 'He still hasn't got back to us.'

'Oh dear,' she said. 'Maybe he didn't quite understand how urgent it was.'

'Of course it isn't exactly a matter of life and death,' said Greg, somehow managing in his tone to imply that it was just that. 'However, there's some urgency to the matter. Perhaps you could contact him again.'

'Yes, of course,' said Claire.

How much longer could she keep this up? Maybe she should just give in and report George missing. After all, he definitely couldn't be at his mother's deathbed, and as far as she knew he didn't have many friends he could have gone to. Unless he had a secret girlfriend somewhere in the background…

Why hadn't she thought of that before? It was the classic explanation for a man's disappearance. He could have had a whole other identity without her suspecting anything. It would be so embarrassing if that came to light, and she couldn't possibly tell anybody from his company, especially not Greg Lawson.

She had no intention of messaging George again yet. If he'd been going to reply, he would have done it the first time. She went through to the hall and put her phone away in the pocket of the waterproof jacket she usually wore for walking Bonzo. There – now she wouldn't be tempted to contact George and, as a bonus, she wouldn't hear the phone ringing if Greg called again either.

Because of this, Claire was standing by the front door when somebody rattled the letterbox. Why hadn't they rung the doorbell? It really annoyed her when people couldn't see what was right in front of their noses…

In the middle of getting cross about this, she flung the door open.

'Yes?' she snapped, and then her brain caught up with her mouth and she realised there was a police officer standing just in front of her, and another one, a woman officer walking up the garden path.

'Mrs Harper? Claire Harper?' said the first one. 'May we come in for a minute?'

'All right, but...'

They introduced themselves and showed their identification. She held the door open for them and showed them to the sitting-room. She realised, glancing round, that it was already not quite as tidy as George would have liked. But that was a good thing, she told herself. It looked more lived-in, more normal. She herself was automatically suspicious of people whose houses were immaculate, and probably these police officers were too.

She moved the interior design magazines off a chair and said,

'Please sit down.'

'Thank you, Mrs Harper.'

She waited for them to tell her why they were here. Was it about George? Had Greg Lawson from his workplace reported him missing, in spite of all her lies about his mother?

'We're looking for Mr George Harper,' said the one who had only spoken to introduce herself. Sergeant Mackenzie. Or was it Macmillan? 'We understand he hasn't been at work for several days.'

'I told Greg Lawson,' she began, and saw them shake their heads.

'He checked out your story about Mr Harper's mother,' said the male officer.

'Apparently she had just left the golf course when he called her.'

'Oh.'

Damn it! That was so like her mother-in-law.

'He said she was excited because she'd gone round in two over par, and it was the best she'd done all year.'

'We wondered why you would have needed to invent a tale about her being on her deathbed,' said the woman officer. Sergeant Mackenzie or Macmillan.

Her tone was casual, almost friendly, but Claire knew this visit meant she was in trouble.

'I didn't want them to know,' she said after a pause. 'George hasn't been home since the end of last week. I didn't want Greg Lawson to know I had no idea where he'd gone.'

'You don't have any knowledge of your husband's whereabouts?' said the male officer. He sounded sceptical, which annoyed her.

'Well I don't have a tracking device on him, that's for sure!' Claire snapped.

The police officers exchanged glances and the woman spoke again.

'He didn't give you any hints about leaving, or about where he might be going?' she asked.

'This is always a difficult question, Mrs Harper, but have you ever thought he might have had a woman friend in his life?'

'No! I've never even suspected that,' said Claire.

She wasn't going to say this to the police officers, but she had seen – saw - George as very much in control of his emotions and actions. He wouldn't have done anything to infringe his self-imposed rules, and playing away from home would definitely have done that.

'So the question is,' said the male officer slowly, 'why haven't you reported him missing yourself, if you didn't know where he'd got to?'

She shrugged helplessly. 'I don't know – I suppose I just thought he was sulking somewhere – we'd had a bit of an argument, just a difference of opinion really. I thought he'd turn up eventually… He isn't the kind of man things happen to. I mean, he wouldn't get himself into a bad situation…'

'Sometimes bad things happen to people when they least expect it, Mrs Harper,' said the woman officer. 'Nobody is immune from accidents or from being in the wrong place at the wrong time.'

They certainly aren't, thought Claire. This was the wrong place at the wrong time, as far as she was concerned. Were the police going to arrest her? What would happen to Bonzo?

Fortunately at that moment the dog nudged the sitting-room door open and trotted into the room, making a fuss of the police officers and, Claire hoped, disarming them. As soon as he stopped, the officers got up and looked as if they might actually leave without taking her with them.

'Please keep us informed, Mrs Harper,' said Sergeant Mackenzie or Macmillan. 'Let us know if you hear anything at all that might help to track him down. A phone call, a message – in fact, do you have his phone number? We might be able to trace him through that, if he's used it at all since he left.'

Claire gave them the number, and her own number in case they needed to call her, and at last they made their way out of the flat, which seemed bigger after they'd gone. She gave Bonzo a pat.

'I guess you saved the day,' she told him. 'They know anybody who loves dogs must be incapable of serious crime.'

That probably wasn't quite true, but she clung to the hope anyway.

Chapter 8 Attack

Jennifer had been to the street where Claire lived, hanging about at the corner until some woman came out of a shop and asked her if she was waiting for somebody. After that, she knew she would have to be a bit more subtle. She searched the neighbourhood for possible dog-walking places. There was the Meadows, of course, but it was mostly quite open, and although they hadn't met all that often, Claire would probably recognise her even in the middle distance. Holyrood Park was another possibility, although a little further away. But once Claire and the dog reached the park, they would have various options about which direction to choose. From where they lived, they might use the Innocent Railway path rather than turning down towards the Palace and the Scottish Parliament, but Jennifer had no idea of how much stamina either Claire or the dog might have.

After walking a couple of the routes, Jennifer wondered if they would really have walked so far. But then, if it hadn't been for all the exercise, Claire would probably have been the size of a house with all her cake consumption. As it was, she had only seemed mildly obese, to use medical language, but her husband had obviously been concerned about her relationship with food in any case.

During one of Jennifer's outings to the park, she thought she saw Claire in the distance with a black dog, but by the time she had got to the place where she'd seen them, they had vanished from sight altogether. Had they gone into the Innocent Railway tunnel? That might have been a good place for an ambush, particularly on a dim, dark day, although Claire might steer clear of it if she was on her own with the dog. Jennifer kept it in mind, silently planning what she would do if she caught them in there. She wondered whether George Harper ever took the dog out himself or even accompanied his wife. She certainly hadn't caught the smallest glimpse of him during the surveillance operation.

After a couple of weeks she had seen Claire and the dog three more times. They tended to go out at different times of day from most of the other dog-walkers, which was probably why Jennifer hadn't seen them at first. It was unlikely anyone would interrupt any action she chose to take.

In between times she stoked her anger by looking at Claire's case notes and recalling every moment of the therapy sessions. Unfortunately this review caused her to develop an irresistible urge to eat a couple of doughnuts, which she scoffed straight from the bag as she followed Claire and the dog. It kept turning and staring, possibly because of the doughnut scent in the air.

On Jennifer's chosen morning the sea mist swirled in the air, chilly and damp. It would clear in patches, tantalizingly, and then more would roll in to fill the gap. But this was ideal for her purposes. She had an idea about Claire's timings now, which enabled her to get ahead of the other woman and her dog on the path and lie in wait.

She stationed herself in bushes not far from the park end of the tunnel. It was almost always quiet there, she had found, especially at this unsocial hour. Having to get up this early would kill her, but with luck after today it would no longer be necessary. Peering through the branches, she saw Claire and the black dog walk past at about their usual time. Now all she had to do was to wait for them to turn and come back the same way. There had hardly been anybody about here any of the times she had come this way.

She shivered, damp seeping through the soles of her shoes from the wet grass. She moved over a few feet, and a bramble caught her sleeve.

It was almost time. She could hear footsteps, then the dog ran past her, quite close by. For a moment she thought he was going to run straight up to her, but she stayed quite still and he only gave her a fleeting glance, as if she were part of the undergrowth. If she stayed her much longer, she might well be.

There were footsteps. Claire wasn't far behind the dog.

Jennifer summoned up all her strength, took her courage in both hands and jumped out on the path right in front of Claire

Only it wasn't Claire at all

She was staring at a complete stranger, a man in a tracksuit. He had obviously been running, but when he saw her, he skidded to a halt a few feet away. She met his baffled gaze with equal bafflement.

'Who the hell are you?' Jennifer demanded.

The madwoman who had jumped out at him from the bushes had the aggressive appearance of somebody planning a physical attack. She actually raised her clenched fists, preparing to punch. Callum stepped back a pace.

'What do you want? I don't have any money or valuables on me.'

'Are you with her?' she demanded.

'Her?'

'That was her dog that just went past. Where is she?'

Callum wanted to say he didn't know what she was talking about, but he thought it best to be a bit more conciliatory, under the circumstances. She had obviously mistaken him for somebody else, but it wouldn't do any good to point that out either. He considered just running away – she didn't look as if she were built for speed – only she was a danger to everybody, including herself, with her menacing expression and raised fists.

'Is there anything I can do to help?' he enquired.

The clenched fists approached again, much too close for comfort.

'I could give you a lift somewhere in my car if you need one,' he said, although the last thing he wanted at this moment was to be stuck in a car with her. 'I'm parked up that way, in Duddingston.'

She was silent, gazing at him from cool grey eyes set in a very pale face, the starkness enhanced by the black hoodie she wore. He was growing uncomfortable with the icy stare, not to mention the fists, of course. She had a couple of rings on her fingers that looked as if they could do some damage.

'There's a van where we could get a coffee – my car's quite close to it. Do you want to walk that way?'

She shook her head almost imperceptibly.

Callum tried again. He couldn't think of anything else to do. Thinking back on what she had said to him about the dog, he realised she had been waiting to ambush another woman at this spot. He couldn't in all conscience leave her here to make another attempt.

'I really don't know anything about this – whatever it is,' he said. 'But I think you need to think seriously about what you want to do.'

At that moment, just as he imagined he might be getting through to her, there was a piercing whistle from somewhere further along the path, followed by a shout.

'Bonzo! Bonzo! Come back here right now.'

'That must be her now,' said the madwoman.

He heard footsteps advancing briskly in their direction. The woman tensed up, presumably getting ready to spring, but he moved to stand in front of her, his hands raised to form a barrier. He hoped this would be enough to prevent her from rushing out on to the path to confront the newcomer. She glared at him fiercely. His intervention seemed to have brought her to her senses, though. As the sound of the footsteps faded away again, she burst into tears, and he realised she wasn't really a madwoman but just somebody who had reached the end of her tether, for whatever reason.

He put his arms round her in an instinctive gesture of comfort, which she didn't resist, and they stood like that until the footsteps had passed them and receded into the distance. With luck the woman and her dog were well out of the way by the time they moved apart.

He thought she might object when he suggested they should walk together along the path towards Duddingston and his car, but all the aggression seemed to have gone from her. He hoped that meant she was regretting her actions.

The route seemed longer now that he was walking instead of running, but eventually she was sitting in the front passenger seat of the car and he was buying both of them a much-needed coffee from the nearby van.

While he was fetching the coffee he had the belated, somewhat uncomfortable thought that if she had really been as unstable as he had at first imagined, she might have tried to drive off and leave him there, except that he had taken the precaution of keeping the key on his person and he sincerely hoped nobody could start the car without it. As far as he knew the days of hot-wiring were well and truly over, though of course you never knew what criminals might think of next.

Callum wound the car windows down to minimize the claustrophobia, and they sat in silence for half an hour or so, taking occasional sips of coffee. He supposed might as well try to get her to talk about it. Not that he was any kind of a counsellor or therapist, of course.

It took a bit of persuasion but after a while she told him about the immense inner struggle she had had to stop using food for comfort, and her subsequent decision to become a therapist, and then, more haltingly, about the woman with the dog who had wrecked her will-power after only a couple of sessions, and about her own fears for the future.

'I don't know if I'll ever be able to offer that kind of eating therapy again – I'd feel like a complete fraud. One bad experience and I've totally given up.'

Callum didn't know anything about eating therapy – he dealt with very different issues in his professional career. Almost the opposite problem, in fact. But he wasn't going to go into that with her right now. He did know a bit about other kinds of addiction, however.

'But won't that make you a better therapist? If you understand about other people's struggles? I bet you've sometimes had to tell people not to think in such extremes. Even if you've given into it today, there's still tomorrow, and so on?'

'Tomorrow and tomorrow and tomorrow,' she said in a mournful voice, and then, to his amazement, she laughed. 'I've probably used up the last of my luck, quoting Macbeth… You're right, though – I have told people that before. I suppose I should just tell myself to try harder next time.'

'Good!' he said. 'Sorry – I'm not any kind of a therapist myself. I've got no right to tell anybody to do anything.'

'Thank you,' she said. 'Attacking Claire Harper would only have made things worse. Much worse. I don't suppose you get the chance to decide between cake or no cake if you go to prison.'

'I shouldn't think you do,' said Callum.

He really ought to get on with his day. He'd be late for work, and there were people depending on him.

As if she had read his thoughts, she said, 'Thanks for the coffee too. I'd better get back. I still have a client to see this morning. Better make the most of it before I have to give it up.'

He had a sudden thought, the kind he'd probably regret later.

'Come and see me if you do decide to stop seeing clients,' he said. 'I might have something for you. In the company, I mean.'

'You don't have to do anything for me,' she said.

'I'd like to help.'

She nodded in acknowledgement and opened the passenger door. She probably didn't believe he was in a position to offer her anything. Or at least, anything she would want to have any part in. He slid a business card out of the glove compartment, got out of the car and handed it to her.

'There. Come to that address if you need to. Don't worry, it's all above-board.'

She didn't even glance at the card but at least she put it away in the pocket of her black hoodie before turning away and jogging off past the coffee van. He watched her with some regret. He would have liked to do something to help her, but she would have to want to be helped.

Chapter 9 Sanctuary

The police came back only two days later. It wasn't such a shock this time, and Claire even thought to offer them coffee, which they politely declined.

'We've heard from Mr Lawson again,' said the male officer.

What were the officers' names again? She hadn't been paying attention the first time, and she didn't want to ask him in case he thought she was planning to make a complaint against him, which surely would have put his back up.

'Oh, yes?' she said.

'He's very concerned about your husband. You haven't heard from Mr Harper yet, by any chance?'

'No, sorry,' mumbled Claire. She didn't know what she was apologising to them for. If anything, they should be apologising to her for not tracking George down, with all the resources they had at their disposal.

'Can you confirm what credit cards and bank cards on him when he disappeared?'

'I suppose he would have had a couple of cards with him,' she said, and gave them as many details as she could recall. 'He usually carried those ones with him when he went to work, as far as I know. And he was last seen at work, wasn't he?'

'As far as we know,' said the male officer, making the simple statement sound a bit threatening. He had a flair for that. 'Unless – is there any chance he came home between the end of the working day and his disappearance? Where were you that day, Mrs Harper?'

She gave a start which she hoped they wouldn't interpret as guilty.

'Um – I suppose I was working at my desk,' she said uncertainly. 'In the back bedroom.'

'You work at home, do you?' said the female officer, sounding surprised.

Claire tried not to frown at the woman. Had she actually lived through the pandemic without realising that millions of people had started working from home then, even if they hadn't before? It wasn't exactly an outlandish thing to do even now.

'Yes,' she said.

'What is it you do, Mrs Harper?' asked the male officer.

She wasn't sure whether he was trying to show a friendly interest, or if he might try and make her perfectly innocent job into something suspicious.

'I help small firms with their social media accounts,' she said.

At this point she didn't really care if they didn't think it was a real job. She just wanted them gone before they intruded even further into her life.

'Does that pay well, then?' enquired the female officer. She glanced round the room as if assessing the value of the furnishings.

Claire shrugged. 'Well enough.'

The male officer coughed. 'This is a bit delicate, but Mr Lawson seemed to think there might have been some trouble between the two of you lately.'

Ha! So George had been discussing her with work colleagues, had he? Probably in the context of the birthday present and her reaction to it. Claire fumed inwardly, while hoping her facial expression didn't reflect this.

'Not really,' she said. 'Nothing serious, anyway.'

'I suppose most married couples go through ups and downs,' said the female officer.

Claire didn't trust the woman, despite her comforting, motherly tone and her words of feminine solidarity.

'Of course,' she said. 'But we agree on most of the important things. I don't know where Mr Lawson got the idea there was anything badly wrong.'

At least that stopped them in their tracks, for the moment. They left soon afterwards. Claire took Bonzo out for an extra walk, twice round the Meadows, but she was still quaking with suppressed panic even after she got back into the flat and locked the door behind her. What if the police came back for a third time? They might still arrest her – they seemed to have been collecting information about the state of her marriage. There was no way they could know she wanted a divorce, though. She was suddenly very glad she hadn't found anybody to confide in. Because if she had wanted to split up and George had refused to co-operate, that might have given her a motive, mightn't it?

A motive – for what?

She stopped with her hand on the kitchen door-handle. Bonzo scratched at the door and whined anxiously, probably worrying that he wouldn't get to his water dish before he expired from thirst.

She opened the door and let him go into the kitchen ahead of her.

Something had happened to George. The police hadn't said what they thought it was, of course, but surely they must have something bad in mind and they didn't imagine he had just left home to live with another woman, or had a breakdown of some kind and caught the first train to nowhere in particular. Although in that case they'd probably be looking for him anyway, in case he did himself some damage en route.

Maybe he had decided he'd had enough of his life here – his life with her – and thought of changing his identity to get away.

Well, in that case she had news for him. She'd have been quite happy to let him go even without the new identity.

Claire didn't sleep well at all that night. Her mind kept jumping to what might happen if the police came back. By morning she had decided she would have to confide in somebody, even if only so that she could ask them to look after Bonzo if she were actually arrested. She had toyed with the idea of booking him into kennels anyway, just in case. But he would have hared it, and to be honest she didn't much like the idea of staying in the flat alone, jumping at every unusual sound and waiting for the police to ring the door-bell again.

Of course she couldn't rely on her mother or sister to do anything to help. They had already tried to distance themselves from her problems. And, working from home as she did, she wasn't sure she knew any of her colleagues well enough to ask them such a huge favour.

It was then, scanning down her email inbox to get some idea of who she'd been in touch with lately, that Claire realised how long it was since she had seen any of her old friends, the ones she had known at university, and in her first job. Of course some of them had left Edinburgh, just as her sister Marilyn had. She vaguely thought Cathy had moved to London a couple of years before to work in television. But what had happened to Pam? And Linda?

Wait a minute – she'd had a card from Linda not long ago.

Claire searched her middle desk drawer, the one where she usually stuffed correspondence she intended to read properly later. Linda had had twins in the autumn! No wonder she'd fallen out of circulation. Goodness knows what had become of Pam, though. She had been determined to remain single and never have children. They met for lunch occasionally. When had they last seen each other?

Claire moved down to the bottom drawer and fished out last year's diary. She had used it mostly for work, recording deadlines and meetings and so on, but there must be a few social engagements in it too. Surely to goodness…

She had to go back to another diary, from the year before last, to find any mention of Pam. They had met for lunch a couple of times, once in May and once in October. The second time must have been a goodbye and good luck lunch for Cathy. Claire remembered it well. George had appeared in mid-afternoon and dragged her out of the restaurant, saying something rude as he did so. Something to do with drinking on work days. How had he even known she was there?

That must be why she hadn't heard from Pam lately.

She put her head in her hands. How typical of George, she realised belatedly, to resent the time she spent with anybody else. It wasn't that he even wanted to do anything with her, either. When they were at home he had taken to watching television on his own in the kitchen rather than with her in the front room. At first she had thought he just didn't like the programmes she preferred, but even after she tried switching on the cricket, or the snooker, instead he would still remain stubbornly in the kitchen. With hindsight, she realised he might have been guarding the biscuit tin so that he could monitor her food intake. Not that there were any interesting biscuits there anyway, because he would only let her buy Rich Teas and plain digestives.

She could eat a whole packet of biscuits right now.

That still wouldn't solve the Bonzo problem, though.

The morning got steadily worse. She fielded another call from Greg Lawson, his tone now even more peremptory, she received an email cancelling a contract with a company she'd enjoyed working with, and then as she drank a third cup of coffee she heard the rattle of the letterbox. With her current run of bad luck, this would probably mean disastrous news of some completely different kind. She sighed, and got up to fetch the post, although she wasn't sure if she could face looking at it.

A couple of brochures from charities – one of the envelopes felt as if it might contain raffle tickets too – and a letter addressed to both her and George, possibly something financial.

It was lunchtime before she felt strong enough to open that one. After lunch, that was, once she had eaten a banana, an apple, a satsuma, two cheese triangles, an oatcake, two doughnuts and a bar of chocolate. She stood at the window and opened the envelope without looking down at it, slid the letter out from inside and then glanced down, eyes half-shut to minimise the impact of what she saw.

The letter was from the bank, and it didn't help at all. Somehow she and George were over a year behind with their mortgage payments.

She slumped down on the top of her desk, her legs suddenly weak and trembling. She thought she might throw up and began to calculate whether she could get to the waste-paper basket in time. What a waste of the two doughnuts that would be! One of them had been the last of the pink iced ones with jam in the middle. She had reached the counter only just in time to buy it before the spotty school kid, arrived, the one she'd seen in the bakery before.

This problematic doughnut-eating scenario suddenly reminded her of Jennifer Ironbridge. This whole thing had started with her, as Claire saw it. With the unwanted birthday present, and her own failure to improve as George had wanted her to.

It was ridiculous to imagine Jennifer could help her now, but Claire couldn't think of anybody else to turn to. Maybe Jennifer could fit her in for some kind of emergency session.

She would take Bonzo with her, both to break the ice and in case the bank sent somebody round that very day to throw her out on the street.

Which no doubt they would do sooner or later, because there was no way she could pay them the amount of money George had failed to hand over. He must have been spending it on something else all along. What had he been thinking?

She calmed herself enough to put on her coat, get Bonzo's lead on, which took longer than it should have done as the dog was beside himself at the thought of going for an extra walk at this time of day, and to leave the flat, carefully locking up behind her. She wasn't going to make it any easier than it needed to be for the bank's minions to get in.

They crossed the Meadows and headed up towards the Old Town, using the quieter streets so that Bonzo didn't get even more excited than he already was.

It wasn't until the two of them stood on Jennifer Ironbridge's doorstep that Claire had second thoughts. But at that point she just told herself that was pointless. Too bad if Jennifer now turned them away. She would just have to think of some other option.

The front door opened. To Claire's surprise and slight consternation, Jennifer herself had come down to greet her instead of simply buzzing her in, as she had done on previous occasions.

The woman took a step backwards when she saw Claire.

'Mrs Ironbridge,' said Claire uncertainly.

'It's Avonbridge,' said Jennifer in a conversational tone, adding, 'as I believe you already know.'

This wasn't a good start.

'But you can call me Jennifer.'

'Oh – thank you.'

Jennifer glanced down at Bonzo. 'Your dog seems to be pleased to see me, anyway.'

Perhaps not surprisingly, she didn't leap at the chance to invite Claire inside.

'I – I need some advice,' said Claire.

'You can book yourself a therapy session if you want. There are plenty of gaps in my calendar.'

'Not that kind of advice.'

Jennifer gave a long sigh, hesitated for a moment and then stood back, holding the heavy door open. 'I suppose you'd better come in.'

Claire dragged Bonzo over the threshold. He didn't seem to want to come in with her, but she certainly wasn't planning to leave him out in the street.

They climbed the stone stairs in silence.

This wasn't exactly how she had hoped things would go.

Chapter 10 Free Therapy

Jennifer hadn't expected her day to get any weirder.

There had been the phone call, first thing that morning.

'Tell you what' Callum had said, 'let's make a bargain.'

She was suspicious, of course. As anybody would have been under the circumstances. After all, he was a complete stranger, or at least as much of a stranger as he could be after she had threatened to attack him and he had talked her down and then bought her a coffee.

'If you promise not to go after that woman again, I can give you a temporary job - maybe permanent. It depends.'

'What sort of a job?'

'Not as a therapist, that's for sure. But we do have some opportunities behind the scenes.'

'Behind the scenes where?'

Jennifer was trying hard to suspend her natural suspicion and to seem completely different from the woman with upraised fists, ready to punch him. Not that she could do so at the other end of the phone line.

'Um – it's a catering operation. Kind of.'

'Catering? You mean I'd have to work with food all day?'

She was able to see the funny side of it, with an effort.

'It's to do with food, as well as other things. It's a community healthy eating project. But you wouldn't have to do any of the actual eating.'

'No food tasting?'

'No. You might have to see some pictures of food. I can't promise you won't.'

She smiled to herself. 'I'll think about it.'

'Let me know as soon as you can if it's a deal. But no going after that woman in the meantime.'

She shook her head. 'I've sort of lost the urge now. Thanks – I think.'

Now here was that woman, on her doorstep.

She regretted letting them in almost at once, when Bonzo jumped up on her favourite chair and looked as if he was going to settle down there. But Claire shooed the dog off the chair, apologised nicely, and she and the animal gazed at Jennifer as if butter wouldn't melt in either of their mouths.

Jennifer shook her head. This wouldn't help her to make up her mind about Callum's offer. But in some indefinable way she felt a bit guilty about not having been able to help Claire, and about the Innocent railway path incident. If she had been able to carry out her initial plan, she might have hurt the other woman, and the dog might have run off and got lost. She wasn't sure which of these possible outcomes disturbed her more.

'Can I get you a coffee? Or tea? I don't have any biscuits, I'm afraid.'

'Coffee would be nice,' said Claire. 'And some water for Bonzo, if it isn't too much trouble. We've walked over from Marchmont.'

When Jennifer returned with the coffee, Claire said, 'I just wish I didn't have biscuits either. Is that the answer, do you think? Not to even have them in the house?'

'It probably helps,' said Jennifer. 'But I assume from what you said that you aren't here for a free eating consultation.'

Claire blushed. 'It's worse than that,' she said. 'I don't have anybody else to talk to.'

'Really? No cosy circle of best friends forever? No sisters you meet every so often over an artistically served afternoon tea?'

'No, actually,' said Claire.

Jennifer was annoyed with herself for using sarcasm so early on in their conversation. She could at least have kept it until Claire had calmed down enough to cope with it.

'My sister's in Barcelona,' Claire added.

Of course she was. And now that the pandemic was on the wane, Claire could pop out there on the next plane if she wanted, and escape from all her tiny little problems.

'George has disappeared,' said Claire. 'And his mother's playing golf, and my mum's busy crafting, and I haven't had time to see any of my old friends for ages.'

Far from calming down, Claire seemed now to be on the verge of tears. Jennifer told herself to be more like the therapist she had been before Claire had ruined her career. She might be able to help the woman to find a way forward through the muddle of her life. She could already see she wasn't going to be able to show Claire the door unless she did something.

'So your husband's gone,' she said slowly. 'Do you mean he's moved out? Run off with another woman? Or just vanished from the face of the earth?'

'Vanished,' said Claire.

The dog, who had seemed to settle on the rug, immediately sat up straight and gave a surprisingly deep bark.

'Shoosh, Bonzo,' Claire told him. She turned back to Jennifer. 'He didn't come home from work one night, and I haven't seen him since. The police have been round twice, and this morning I opened a letter from the bank and found out that George hasn't been paying the mortgage for months.'

'Oh, no!' said Jennifer. She hadn't been altogether sympathetic with Claire over George Harper's disappearance – the man was old enough and ugly enough to look after himself, as her mother would have said, although to be fair she didn't know how ugly he was. But not paying the mortgage was unforgiveable.

'You didn't know there was anything wrong?' she enquired, conscious that her tone had softened.

Claire shook her head. 'It was silly of me. I should have looked at the bank statements myself, but he always got to them first, and I thought everything was fine. He gets a good salary and I've had plenty of work, although I'm freelance. We always had enough for a nice holiday and good Christmas presents. I don't know what's been going on.'

Jennifer's first thought was that George must have been spending the mortgage money on supporting a second family, but maybe that was too simple. She didn't want to come right out with that theory in any case, because Claire probably wasn't ready to hear it.

'The HR people from his work have been calling every other day too,' Claire continued. 'They haven't seen him either.'

'So he disappeared on his way home from work, then? Have the police checked with public transport and cctv and so on?'

'I assume they have. We haven't gone into the detail. I was worried they suspected me. They implied he might have come home from work and then disappeared.'

Her voice trembled.

'Could he have gone home without you seeing or hearing him?' said Jennifer.

Claire shook her head. 'That's very unlikely. I would have been working in the back bedroom. The flat isn't that big, and George isn't somebody who creeps about. He'd have been much more likely to barge in on me and interrupt a Zoom call.'

'But maybe if he hadn't wanted you to hear him....'

'I suppose that's just about possible. But Bonzo would have heard something. He usually scratches at the bedroom door when he hears George in the hall.'

Jennifer thought this over. It was starting to seem as if she should have focused her surveillance efforts on George Harper rather than his wife. He obviously had a lot more to hide. The information from the bank made it more likely that he had chosen to disappear than that he had met with an accident or got accidentally mixed up in gang warfare.

'You've got to tell the police about the mortgage,' she said firmly 'They need to know he was in financial trouble.'

'But won't they just think I knew about it already and lost my temper and attacked him or - or took out a contract on him?'

Jennifer tried not to laugh. Despite her eating problem, Claire really didn't look robust enough to be able to much damage to a fully-grown man, though of course she might have managed to push him into traffic if he'd lost his balance. Only in that case his disappearance would no longer be a mystery.

Instead of commenting on that aspect of the situation, she said,

'Where would you have got the money to take out a contract, if the two of you couldn't even pay the mortgage between you?'

'It was up to George to pay the mortgage,' said Claire crossly. 'And the electricity. I just paid for the internet and food shopping out of my account.'

At least the woman was no longer on the verge of tears.

'Still,' said Jennifer patiently, 'you probably didn't make enough to pay anybody to harm him, did you?'

'I suppose not,' said Claire. 'The police might still think so, though… What am I going to do?'

'You could try and track him down,' said Jennifer. 'If you can find him, then it won't be anything to do with the police any more… Are you sure you don't have any idea where he could have got to?'

'No, of course I haven't!' Claire snapped. She paused and apologised at once. 'Sorry, I know this isn't your fault. It's just that I've never even imagined this happening. I only thought of it happening the other way round, if you see what I mean. I wanted to split up, but I hadn't done anything about it yet.'

'Maybe he wanted the same,' said Jennifer, following a long pause during which she fervently hoped Claire hadn't divulged this to the police. 'Maybe he'd been wanting the same thing for a while, and he'd made his own plans. With a bit of forward planning he could even have created a fake identity or made a new life for himself somewhere else. That could be why he wasn't paying the mortgage – he had other expenses elsewhere.'

Claire jumped up from the chair so suddenly that she scared Bonzo, and he ran round in circles, barking. The effort of calming him down seemed to take the edge of the anger she must inevitably have felt.

'Oh, dear,' she said, still patting the dog's head, 'I forgot he was here, sorry.'

Jennifer resisted the temptation to roll her eyes. In her opinion, if Claire hadn't spent her time apologising for her mere existence, she probably wouldn't have married George Harper in the first place and consequently wouldn't have had any eating problems or, more pertinently, missing husband problems.

She hadn't asked to be the recipient of Claire's confidences at this point – in fact, she had tried to take steps not to be – but now that they were both here having this conversation, she felt bound to do her best to help. Had Claire even searched George's belongings, or tried to access his emails or social media? Presumably the police had phone records, but could Claire somehow get her hands on these? There were various possibilities to explore. They weren't at the end of the road by any means.

Jennifer resisted the temptation to offer Claire a bed for the night, partly because of Bonzo, but mostly because of their earlier history as client and therapist, although they had definitely progressed some way beyond that now. Instead she advised the other woman to get a good night's sleep.

'Things will seem better after that,' she lied as she ushered woman and dog out and closed the door firmly behind them. 'You'll get a bit more perspective.'

Of course she couldn't imagine Claire's problems would magically become easier to solve after a few hours' sleep. Unless maybe her sister flew in from Barcelona unexpectedly to offer assistance, or her mother gave up crafting for five minutes to pay attention. Both these possibilities seemed rather remote. If the family hadn't rallied round during what Jennifer now knew must have been difficult years for Claire, they weren't likely to think of doing so now.

She mustn't forget to get back to Callum in the morning about the job either. There was no point in offering helpful advice to Claire while ignoring her own situation.

Maybe tomorrow or the next day she could either steer Claire in the direction of looking for evidence of George's activities in the immediate past, or even go to their flat herself one evening and lead the search, if it couldn't be avoided.

That would be absolutely the last resort, she told herself.

Chapter 11 DNA

The police phoned one morning a few days later, before coming round to the flat again. Were they just being polite and considerate, or was there some reason why they had warned her of their visit? Claire had recovered from the panic that had sent her over to Jennifer's that evening, but she still felt anxious about what the police wanted. Might it be bad news? Or were they planning to arrest her? What about Bonzo?

'Mrs Harper. This is my colleague, Detective Inspector Wood.'

This was different. He was obviously a more senior officer than the two who had come round before. Claire took a mental note of his name and tried to remain calm, at least on the surface. Underneath, of course, her brain was bubbling away like an underwater volcano.

She took them into the front room, and the woman officer she had met before advised her to sit down.

'You may find this latest development a bit upsetting, Mrs Harper.'

The three of them sat down.

'What is it?' said Claire in a small voice, glancing from one to the other.

'We've found something that could be relevant to Mr Harper's disappearance,' said the detective inspector. 'We now have to ask you for access to his personal possessions, or those he left here.'

'You haven't thrown anything out, have you?' said the woman officer suddenly.

The inspector seemed annoyed with his colleague for interrupting. 'There's also the matter of dental records. Do you know the name of your husband's dentist?'

'His dentist?'

Dental records. Wasn't how they identified…? Claire felt light-headed. She hoped she wouldn't have to get to her feet in the near future. If she attempted it, she knew she would either fall to the floor and injure herself or throw up on the inspector's shoes. Either way, it wouldn't be a good look.

'Maybe you went to the same dentist?' said the inspector.

'Yes, but I'm not sure if he'd been there for a while,' said Claire. 'They were closed for a long time, and…'

'I expect they'll still have his records, though,' said the inspector.

She gave him the name and address of the dentist.

'You can look wherever you like in the flat,' she told them. 'What sort of thing were you thinking of? Clothes and so on?'

The inspector nodded. 'And hairbrush, toothbrush, that kind of thing,' he said gently. 'You might like to come with us.'

'No, it's fine,' said Claire. She wondered if she would have been better to have a friend or even a lawyer with her in case they planted evidence or something, but surely they only did that in television crime dramas and not in real life.

He nodded to the woman officer and they got up and went away, presumably to search.

'Would you like coffee?' said Claire when they came back, belatedly remembering to act the part of the gracious hostess that her mother had fondly imagined she might become.

Not that she was in her mother's world any longer. This was an alternate universe in which husbands vanished and wives were suspected of doing away with them. Where human remains were found that could only be identified from DNA. The woman officer had brought in a plastic bag which must contain the items they'd been looking for.

'No, thank you, Mrs Harper... I believe you gave my officers an account of your whereabouts around the last time you saw your husband?'

She wished he would stop referring to George as her husband. It made her feel as if he had been one of her belongings that she should have taken more care of.

'Yes, I think I did.'

'Can I trouble you to go through it again?' he asked. 'Just in case we missed any relevant facts.'

Or in case I slip up and change my story, and you decide to arrest me, she thought wildly.

The inspector nodded from time to time as she went through it. She didn't suppose for a moment that he was nodding in agreement with her account. For all she knew, his nods were a secret sign to the constable that his suspicions were justified.

'So you last saw him that morning when he went to work.'

'I didn't really see him even then,' said Claire. 'He was in a rush – he just called to me before he went out.'

'Can you tell me any more, Mrs Harper, about the nature of the problems you and your husband experienced?'

'As I said before, there weren't any major disagreements.'

'Not about money, for instance?' said the inspector.

What was he getting at? She and George hadn't argued about money at all – well, not very much. Except that she would rather he'd spent the money on something nice for her birthday instead of the therapy sessions. She didn't want to mention therapy, though. For one thing, it would make it sound as if she were on the verge of something worse than being a little too fond of cake, and for another, she had started to see Jennifer as a friend and not a therapist. Even if this feeling turned out to be an illusion, for the moment Jennifer represented a sanctuary where the police couldn't get to her.

'I don't remember any major arguments about money,' she said after a pause.

Had the pause been too long? Would it make them suspicious?

'Look,' she said, 'why don't you tell me exactly what you're doing here? You've found something – somebody. It – he – is in such a bad state that you can't identify him. What makes you think it's George? Where did you find it – him?'

She couldn't really think of some unidentifiable set of human remains as her missing husband. He had been perfectly fine when he had left the flat that morning. She would have known if he'd got involved in something dangerous, wouldn't she? Even if he hadn't told her anything, she would have sensed something badly wrong. People like them didn't get into this kind of situation.

'Yes, we've found something,' said the inspector. 'That's all I can say for the moment. We aren't sure the discovery has anything to do with Mr Harper, but we have to check against all known missing persons. I must warn you that if we do identify the – discovery – as Mr Harper, we shall have to ask you further questions.'

He got up to leave.

'Can you please sign for these belongings, Mrs Harper?' said the woman officer in a low voice. 'You'd better have a look at what I've got in here, just so you know.'

It was oddly poignant, looking at George's old brush – but Claire halted, her pen poised over the form.

'That's Bonzo's brush, not George's.'

'So these are dog hairs on it? There's no chance that your husband used it too?'

'He wouldn't dream of it,' said Claire with confidence. 'I suppose DNA would tell you that eventually though.'

'It would,' said the inspector with a faint smile. 'In that case, did Mr Harper normally take his hairbrush to work with him?'

'I don't think so,' said Claire.

'Maybe you could have a look for it, if you're sure you haven't thrown it out,' said the inspector. 'And see if anything else is missing... That could be very helpful, potentially.'

'I don't suppose the toothbrush belongs to the dog too?' said the woman officer.

Chapter 12 Seeing the Black Dog

Jennifer wasn't sure if she had done the right thing in accepting Callum's offer, even if it was only on a trial basis, and the first few days of her employment made her less sure, if anything. She seemed to have got off on the wrong foot with the other clerk who shared her office, and there had a narrow escape from chaos in the kitchen when she wandered in there and offered unsolicited advice on ethically sourced ingredients.

She sensed from Callum's manner that he now had serious doubts about her. Maybe he was already agonising over whether to give her yet another chance or not. Control of the situation seemed to be slipping away from her, something she knew from past experience might drive another unhealthy eating binge.

It was partly because of this feeling that she entered the kitchen again, this time to enquire about the use of additives in the ready-meals they served up to vulnerable members of the community.

'I'm sorry,' she told Callum when he challenged her on her activities. 'I just wanted to be sure...'

He sighed, running his fingers through his hair and causing it to stand up on end, which gave him the look of a mad professor.

'It's taken me half an hour to persuade the chef to stay on,' he said. 'What didn't you understand the last time I said you weren't to interfere in the kitchen?'

'It's just that I think the food they prepare should be as good as it can be!' she said. 'What don't you understand about that?'

He frowned at her. 'Maybe you should count to ten before you speak in future.'

She folded her arms and glared back. 'If you're going to fire me, why not just do it right now and save us both a lot more hassle?'

'Do you want to leave?'

This time she did count to ten.

Then she said, 'Not really, no. This is far more worthwhile than my nutritional therapy business. I can only help one or two people at a time with that kind of thing. Your operation helps a lot more than that.'

He nodded. 'Once you've been here a bit longer and found out how it all works, I'll let you discuss the food content with the chef – but only if you're good.'

'All right.'

He sat down suddenly at his desk. She supposed he was tired of arguing with her. She didn't blame him.

'It's not your fault,' he said, staring up at her. 'The chef's a bit over-sensitive, and I should've brought him into line before now. I just haven't faced up to it. I've been waking up in the night wondering how to start a conversation with him but I'm a bit baffled.'

He lowered his head and stared at the top of the desk instead.

'Why do you think you feel like that?'

Jennifer had unconsciously reverted to her therapist mode. It was either that or stroke his hair and tell him he was doing fine, which even she knew would be inappropriate.

'I don't know,' he muttered.

'If he's so good at his job, does he make you feel inadequate?'

He jerked his head up much too quickly and must have cricked his neck. 'Ouch!'

He massaged the back of his neck with one hand and pretended to move the mouse with the other.

'You aren't all right, are you?' said Jennifer.

'I'm fine,' he said.

'Just tell me how you feel. You can say anything you like. I won't be shocked.'

'The black dog!' he exclaimed, staring straight ahead.

'Well, if that's how you like to think of it,' she began.

'No, it's really a black dog. There. In the doorway. How did it get in?'

'Oh dear,' she said, and stroked his hair after all. 'It's worse than I thought.'

There were footsteps – human – in the corridor and Jennifer glanced round to see Claire run n past the open doorway.

'It's her again!' said Callum. 'The woman we saw in the woods. She had a black dog then too.'

'I wonder if you've ever considered medication,' said Jennifer, frowning. 'It can be quite effective, especially for hallucinations.'

'No, really. If you go out in the corridor maybe you'll see her. And the dog.'

'I wonder if a change of diet would…?'

Callum got up from his chair, walked over to the doorway and out to the corridor – and the black dog almost sent him flying on its return from wherever it had been.

He grabbed at its trailing lead and dragged it into the office so that she could see it.

'There!'

'Oh, dear,' she said. 'I'm sorry. It didn't occur to me to take it literally. Churchill, you know…'

'Yes, I know about Churchill and black dogs.'

Claire ran past again.

'Oi!' Jennifer called. 'We've got Bonzo!'

She came back more slowly and gave them a huge smile. 'Thank you.'

Callum handed over the dog's lead. He turned back to Jennifer.

'Do you know this dog?'

'It's Bonzo,' said Jennifer. 'And this is Claire,' she added a bit reluctantly. 'I don't know what she's doing here.'

'I'm Callum,' he told Claire, 'I'm in charge, and this is a food preparation area. We can't have animals rampaging round the building. I'm going to have to ask you to leave.'

'Sorry,' said Claire. 'I need to speak to Jennifer urgently.'

'I'm afraid you'll have to do that outside working hours,' said Callum.

'I can meet you at lunchtime if it really is urgent,' said Jennifer.

Claire nodded. Now that Jennifer looked at her more closely, it was clear something must be badly wrong. Had the police tracked down George, and was it bad news?

'I'll wait outside. On the bench near the bus stop,' said Claire.

'It's started to rain,' said Callum. 'You'd better go along to the café on the corner and talk there. Go now,' he urged Jennifer, 'and get this over with.'

'Thank you,' said Claire.

'Thanks,' said Jennifer, although she wasn't quite clear what she was thanking him for. She was almost certain Claire was about to suck her even further into the maelstrom of her chaotic life.

'Just do it,' he said. 'And get the dog out of here before he causes any more metaphorical misunderstandings.'

Chapter 13 Detective Work

'Right, then,' said Jennifer as soon as they came in at the front door. 'Where are we going to start?'

Claire had explained to Jennifer over their snack lunch about the police and the toothbrush and the dog brush. Doing so had helped to calm her down quite a lot. Maybe she shouldn't have been quite so quick to abandon Jennifer's therapy sessions. Though the long walk with Bonzo she had taken after lunch while she waited for Jennifer's working day to be over seemed to have helped too.

Left to her own devices, Claire would have started by fetching a cup of coffee, and maybe a chocolate biscuit, and sitting down at her desk to think. She would then almost certainly have opened her laptop and glanced through her inbox, not really meaning to deal with any work but hoping something so urgent would have come up that she would have to plunge into it and ignore any real-life problems.

She realised that her tendency to do this was probably why she was stuck dealing with other people's social media while Jennifer had her own thriving business, or at least she seemed to have had a business until very recently.

'You aren't really going to give up doing therapy, are you?' she asked.

Jennifer frowned. 'Let's just stick to the task in hand, will we? Now, has George left any of his phones or computers here in the flat, or would he have taken them to work with him that last day?'

'He only had one phone, and he kept it with him. Computers – mm, yes. He works from home a couple of days a week, and he has a laptop for that. I don't think he usually took it into the office with him, though.'

'Did he have a separate office where he worked?'

Jennifer was being very patient. She had the air of a nursery school teacher leading a child through the steps they needed to accomplish something very simple.

'In the flat? Well, he used the dining alcove,' said Claire. 'It's this way.'

The dining alcove was a dim, dark corner sandwiched between the front room and the kitchen. It had no windows of its own, but there were glass double doors leading to the kitchen, so at least some light filtered in that way. Claire had sometimes wondered why George had chosen to work in such cramped surroundings. After all, he could have taken over the front room if he'd wanted. She had suggested that option to him several times during the first lockdown, when they'd both been working full-time in the flat.

She pushed that thought aside and concentrated on her husband's murky little workspace. There was nothing on the desktop apart from the essential lamp. George's small compact printer sat on one of the built-in shelves next to the desk.

'Oh, he'll have locked the laptop away,' said Claire. She slid a hand under the wood of the desktop and came up with a key. 'He thought this was a big secret but I saw him using it once.'

'It isn't all that secure,' said Jennifer.

'He thinks I'm stupid, you see.'

Claire leaned down and opened the top drawer.

'There. All the others will open now... My goodness!'

She was staring at a bundle of banknotes stashed inside the drawer she had just opened.

'Where did that come from? I wonder how much there is.'

She reached towards the money, but Jennifer stopped her at the last moment.

'I wouldn't touch that if I were you. The police might be interested.'

'Oh, yes, of course! Should we have left the desk to them to search?'

'I don't think so,' said Jennifer. 'But you don't want to leave your fingerprints all over the money, do you?'

'I suppose not. Will we try the next drawer? It's bigger. Maybe that's where he put the laptop.'

The next drawer was empty, and so was the bottom one. What could he have done with the laptop?

'He must have taken it with him after all,' she said uncertainly.

'Is there anywhere else he might have left it? In the front room?'

They came out of the alcove and glanced round the room. It seemed oddly cold and unwelcoming, Claire thought, trying to see it through Jennifer's eyes. George had insisted on only using neutral colours in the décor. Maybe he'd already been looking ahead to a time when they would have to leave the flat because he hadn't been paying the mortgage. But that would mean this whole thing was premeditated, and she didn't want to believe that. He had thought of giving her a present on her birthday, hadn't he? Even if it was something he must have known she didn't want.

'What's that?' said Jennifer suddenly.

'What?'

'Look – there's an envelope propped up against the tv.'

'No!' said Claire. She didn't want to see the envelope and certainly had no wish to open it and find out what was inside.

Jennifer glanced sideways at her. 'Haven't you seen it before?'

'I don't know if I've been in here for a day or two… Wait a minute! I brought the police in to talk to them. I'm almost sure the envelope wasn't here then. Does that mean he came back today – while I was out?'

As Claire hung back, Jennifer strode forward and picked up the envelope. She thrust it under Claire's nose.

'Is this his writing?'

Claire nodded miserably.

She wasn't sure why she should be miserable, unless it was because he'd come back when she had imagined he'd left for good. A man who had adopted a new identity wouldn't have revisited his old one, would he?

'Aren't you going to open it?' asked Jennifer.

'I don't know.'

Jennifer sighed. 'You're not going to drag out this Schrödinger's cat moment, are you?'

'I don't know what you're talking about.'

But after a further tantalising pause, Claire snatched the envelope and tore it open. She pulled out the sheet of paper inside so fast that she ripped the corner off it. She slowed down a little. She really wanted to tear the whole thing up without reading it. That would serve him right.

But she was an adult. She unfolded the sheet and read what he had written. Then, in a very considered, adult way, she began to tear it into very small pieces and scatter them about her feet.

Slightly to her surprise, Jennifer just watched without comment until Claire dusted the last fragments off her hands. Then she began an ironic slow clapping. Bonzo, who had also been watching but more anxiously, barked once and then fell silent.

'Don't say anything,' Claire told her.

'I take it the police don't need to be involved any more,' said Jennifer.

'He's on his way to Barcelona,' said Claire. 'To live with my sister. He hopes I'll understand in time. I won't, of course. He knows I might be a bit short of money, so he's left me some cash in the desk... At least it isn't my mother he's going off with.'

She gave a short laugh.

'What a slimy worm,' said Jennifer.

'Yes.'

'He should have had the nerve to tell you face to face.'

'Yes. I'm kind of surprised my sister didn't mention it when I last spoke to her, though.'

'Yes.'

Claire realised, very much to her surprise, that Jennifer was probably the best person she could have had with her at this particular moment.

She sighed, but not in a sad or long-suffering way. It was more like the release of a tension that had gripped her for longer than she knew. It must have been caused by George, all along.

'I suppose I'd better tell the police I know where he is,' she said.

She knew it was just the first of many awkward calls she would have to make. Best to start straight away, then.

'It's a pity in a way, though,' she added thoughtfully. 'I could've done with his life insurance payout.'

'For goodness' sake don't say that to the police!' said Jennifer.

'I won't.'

'Is there anything I can do?' said Jennifer.

'Do you want to make us both some coffee? I think we need it.'

'Is there any cake?' enquired Jennifer.

She caught Claire's eye and they both laughed.

'There isn't any cake,' said Claire primly. She glanced down at the shreds of George's letter. 'I've got bananas and apples and pears and strawberries. And if you want to gnaw on a carrot, there are some of those too.'

The End

~~~~~~

Deadly Embrace

She was going to switch off the light again. He knew it. He waited... Ten, nine, eight....

'I'll just switch off this one. You won't need the overhead light as well as the lamp and the telly.'

He didn't reply, only frowned at the television screen as if concentrating deeply. He heard the click of the switch.

'See you later, then,' she added. 'Don't wait up.'

It was a joke, of course, because she knew he almost never moved from the sofa bed at any time of the day or night anyway. Or at least she thought she knew. Evening classes, eh? Two could play at that game. He listened with half an ear to her progress towards the front door, and with half his attention on the news programme he liked.

'... so we used to call that kind of stalemate a deadly embrace,' the computer expert on television was saying. 'Of course, nowadays we have ways of avoiding it....'

As soon as she had left the house, he had his tablet up and running. He had reached lesson six of the home electrics internet course, and it was starting to get very interesting indeed.

'This is where you have to use extreme caution,' said the presenter brightly, pulling a handful of wires away from the wall and attacking them with pliers. 'Remember, always disconnect the circuit from the mains supply before you start on the project. You'll usually find the circuit breakers, if you have them, right by the electricity meter. Can't miss them.'

'And of course,' he continued with a broad grin, 'don't put the power back on until you've completely finished. No wires sticking out. No loose screws.'

He must be thinking about how stupid somebody would have to be to make that kind of mistake.

Alone with the tablet, the man nodded. You'd have to be stupid, or irresponsible – or just plain desperate to break free of the deadly embrace.

'We have ways of avoiding it,' he said to himself.

He was still lying on the sofa bed, eyes closed, a smug little smile on his lips, by the time she came back. She stood there for a moment. He could feel her malevolent stare. His smile almost began to widen, but he controlled it with an effort. She couldn't switch off the light again because it was already off, but her urge to do it was almost tangible.

It wasn't just the light switch. She had a way of looking at him that somehow encapsulated all she felt: disappointment, mostly, about how her life had turned out, and resentment, that went without saying because she never actually voiced it, and sometimes just a glint of something more sinister. If she had ever bothered really to look at him these days, he guessed she would have detected the same toxic mix of emotions. A deadly embrace, indeed.

They had only stayed together because neither of them would take the initiative to leave. Until now.

In the middle of the following week, he was forced to leave the sofa bed for a few hours to attend a hospital appointment. Someone had arranged transport for him, but it came far too early and he had to wait for a long time to see the consultant. As usual, the doctors said he needed to get out and about more, and tried to persuade him he would like to go to a day centre once a week. He suspected her of being behind this idea.

'Or there's the Men's Shed group round at the community centre,' said one of the woman doctors eagerly.

'What would I do there?'

'Well, you'd meet other men – retired, mostly – and make things. Just like in a real shed.'

'Make things?'

'You know, use your hands a bit. Give you something to think about.'

He had plenty to think about at home, and plenty of things to keep his hands occupied, too. They would have been amazed if they'd known.

He sensed she had been in the room when he got back. Little things had been moved. The television remote was in a different place from usual. The television itself had been swung round at a slightly different angle. A cup he had left on the bookshelves had vanished. A coffee stain on the table was gone. Ha! There wouldn't be any more of this changing things around soon. She hadn't switched off the telly, though, so that was something. She must have learned that much about him after thirty years of stalemate.

That evening, he waited impatiently for her to get ready for her class.. It took her a while this time. Was she dressing up for the benefit of the instructor he suspected was the reason for her perfect attendance? He sniffed the air for traces of perfume.

She was running late. Hmph. Primping and preening right up to the last minute, no doubt.

She came into the room and it was just as he had imagined, Nice top, skinny jeans, dash of perfume. Heels. She didn't look too bad for her age. He felt a pang of sorrow for what he had to do, but her next words squashed it down flat in his chest like a burst balloon.

'We've finished the actual course now. So we're going on a night out. One of the others is picking me up in a bit.'

'Good,' he said.

She gave him a funny look, but he knew it couldn't mean anything.

'I forgot to ask,' he said, pretending he really wanted to know. 'What was the course about?'

'Oh, nothing you'd be interested in.'

'Go on, try me.'

'Well, it was a kind of do-it-yourself thing, if you must know. Specially for women. Electrical safety, that kind of thing.'

'For women, eh?' he said, thinking the course instructor was on to a good thing there.

'The instructor's a woman too,' she said.

The doorbell rang, and she turned to leave the room.

'I'll just switch the light off,' she said. 'Can't have you dazzled by it.'

'Oh, don't bother, dear. I'll be fine.'

'Oh, go on, I know you like it a bit dim.'

At the last minute he wanted to dive across the room and stop her. But it was too late.

Without even looking, she reached over to the light switch, knowing exactly where it was because she had done this so many times before. She touched it.

Click! Bang! Flash!

'Ow!' She slumped against the wall and gradually slid to the floor. Her eyes were still open, wide with panic. 'Help – me!' she gasped. She tried to put a hand up to her chest, but somehow her limbs were no longer functioning as they should.

He couldn't look at her any longer, and in any case, it was time for his favourite news programme. He turned and picked up the remote control.

Just before he pressed the button, he thought she gasped out a few more words.

'Don't – do – that.'

Bang! Flash!

He was thrown back on the sofa with some force as the television exploded in front of him, its screen shattering and flinging needle-sharp fragments around the room. He was only hazily conscious that one of the fragments had embedded itself in his chest. He couldn't breathe by then, anyway, so it didn't really matter.

He never even heard the rattle of her dying breath. After a while the doorbell rang again, its peal resonating urgently through the house, but neither of them got up to answer its summons.

In Search of a Saint (a Pitkirtly origin myth)

Because it turned out that, due to circumstances beyond anyone's control, the contents of the filing cabinets had to be rearranged, a previously overlooked folder came to light, and Christopher took it over to his desk for a closer look.

He was always up for a morning spent in poking about in local history, but particularly when the finance department at the Council were breathing down his neck for the Folk Museum attendance figures, despite everyone knowing the place had been closed for almost the whole of the last financial year.

It was just bad luck that Amaryllis happened to come and bother him soon after he had got started.

'What's this, then?' she enquired. 'More mouldy old documents? Is it the McCallum letters again?'

He knew she and most of the other people who frequented Christopher's office thought he would probably spend the rest of his working life trying to get through the McCallum letters. It seemed to have become a standing joke among his friends.

'It isn't actually,' he said with dignity. 'This file came in separately, from the people at the Bowling Club. They seemed to think it might be of general interest.'

'Ooh, yes!' exclaimed Amaryllis. 'Does it give the low-down on El Presidente's rise to power?'

El Presidente was a local politician who had once been the President of the Bowling Club.

'Not so far,' said Christopher. 'It's mostly membership lists – oh, and here's an old map for the collection.'

He unfolded the map and spread it out on his desk. She came round to his side and peered at it.

'It's a bit faint,' she complained. 'Why is there a cross in the middle? X marks the spot. Is there pirates' treasure buried under there?'

He looked more closely at the place she indicated. 'It looks as if – wait…'

He delved in the top drawer of his desk and brought out a magnifying glass.

'That's funny. It seems to be a church symbol.'

She frowned. 'Not treasure, then.'

'Not earthly treasure anyway,' said Christopher, laughing. He didn't subscribe to organised religion any more than she did, but it was fun to try and wind her up a bit.

He leaned over the map again. There was some faded brown script next to the church symbol. St Something. But if he was reading the map correctly, it was nowhere near either of the two existing churches. It must just represent the remains of one that had long since been demolished.

He held the magnifying glass over the small lettering. 'St Kertlan? Is there any such saint?'

'Don't ask me!' said Amaryllis. 'Weren't there lots of weird saints in the Celtic church? Jemima was rambling on about it one night just recently in the pub.'

'I don't know much about them,' said Christopher.

'Google is your friend,' said Amaryllis, and leaned over him to switch on the computer on the desk. 'I bet some Celtic church nerd will have them all listed out with dates and miracles.'

'It looks as if this church was in the middle of the bowling green,' said Christopher as they waited for the machine to boot up.

'Funny place to put it.'

'I think it was the other way round. The bowling green was built over the church. Or on the site of it.'

'You don't say.'

They searched for saints of the Celtic church and found St Kertlan in some nerd's sub-list of doubtful saints.

'I suppose that means they weren't as saintly as all that,' suggested Amaryllis.

'I think it means their existence is doubtful,' said Christopher.

'I see his special power was holding back the tide, like some kind of dodgy King Canute,' she said, still gazing at the computer screen.

'I suppose that's as likely as anything,' said Christopher.

'Maybe we can get someone to dig up the bowling green and find it,' said Amaryllis. She was starting to sound a lot more interested. Of course from her point of view the more disruption and excitement it would cause, the better.

'I wonder if there's anything else about it in the file,' said Christopher, leafing through the other documents. 'Look, somebody's written a history of the bowling club.'

He held up an amateurish looking booklet with a cover showing Pitkirtly bowling club headquarters in unlikely shades of green and brown, with a couple of bowlers standing self-consciously in the middle of the picture.

He opened the booklet and scanned the text quickly.

'It doesn't start until 1921,' he said. 'Part of the postwar reconstruction work, I suppose.'

'Perhaps they'll have centenary celebrations any day now. They could organise a dig as part of that.'

'It seems highly unlikely that anything's happening, though,' remarked Christopher. 'You'd have thought there would have been posters up or something.'

'Maybe they're keeping it secret.'

'That wouldn't be like them.'

'Do we know anyone with Bowling Club connections?' she said.thoughtfully.

At that moment Christopher's colleague, Kyle, happened to enter the office.

Amaryllis's eyes narrowed. 'Does your uncle still belong to the Bowling Club?' she asked him.

'No – we can't ask him!' said Christopher.

Kyle approached the desk and saw the map.

'A map of Pitkirtly!' he exclaimed. Just as Amaryllis had, he homed in on the church symbol, adding, 'What's that? It isn't anywhere near either of the churches.'

'It's St Kertlan's,' Amaryllis told him. 'But we'd need an archaeological dig to find it.'

He shook his head. 'My uncle will kill me if he finds out I've told you, but...'

'Told us what?' Amaryllis prompted.

'Now you've got so close, I'm going to have to,' said Kyle. 'Otherwise I expect you'll find a way of getting in there at night and digging all over the place.'

'What?' said Christopher.

Amaryllis's eyes gleamed.

'Tell us everything.'

Later that same day, Kyle led them on an expedition to the Bowling Club. Well, theoretically he was the one in the lead, but actually Amaryllis was operating him as surely as if he had been a puppet. Kyle used an impressively enormous key to open the gate to the grounds owned by the club.

'My uncle doesn't know I have this,' he said. 'I thought it would come in useful one day.'

Christopher wasn't sure that 'useful' was the right word. 'Dangerous' and 'illegal' seemed more apposite to him.

They paused on a paved path behind the actual green, and Kyle got down on his hands and knees and levered up one of the largest paving stones. Amaryllis shone her torch downwards into the black hole that opened up.

'What's down there?' said Christopher uneasily.

'Come on down and you'll see,' said Kyle.

'After you,' said Christopher. He wasn't entirely happy about descending into the darkness.

'All right.'

But once they had climbed down the stone steps that were set into the downward slope, Kyle reached round behind him and flicked a switch. The interior of the space was flooded with light.

It was roughly the size and shape of a small chapel, and there were stone benches angled towards a large stone cross at the far end.

'Wow!' breathed Amaryllis. 'Is this it? St Kertlan's church?'

'Not really,' said Kyle, his matter-of-fact tone slicing into the chilly air like a knife into butter that had just come out of the fridge. 'But it's the closest thing to it.'

'What do you mean?' said Christopher.

'It's a reconstruction on the same site, or as near as dammit,' said Kyle. 'St Kertlan,' he continued in the voice of a teacher educating a couple of ignorant pupils, 'was one of the earliest Christian saints, and he came to Pitkirtly, though it wasn't called that in those days, well before St Serf appeared in Culross. Only there was nobody much to write anything down about him, and the only useful thing he seems to have done was to banish a huge sea monster from the waters about here. There's a tradition that the sea monster went north after that, possibly to Loch Ness. St Kertlan had made Pitkirtly too hot for it…. But very few people know about this.'

'Don't tell me,' said Amaryllis, 'only members of the Bowling Club and their families and friends. And friends of their friends. And almost everyone in town except us.'

Kyle shook his head. 'No – far from it. It's a secret only handed down in a few families. Through the generations. Centuries before the Bowling Club was set up, there was a rudimentary bowling green on this site, and my ancestors owned it but allowed the townspeople to play bowls on it on the first Saturday of each month. We've got a book about it at home. When I overheard my uncle talking about St Kertlan, I read all about him.'

'Wow!' said Amaryllis again. 'What a pointless thing to have handed down – isn't it?'

'There's something quite – magnificent about the pointlessness, though,' said Christopher.

'A magnificent legacy,' agreed Kyle. 'Come on then, we'd better get out of here before the cleaners arrive.'

'The cleaners know about it?' said Christopher.

'No – but they go round in the clubhouse every Thursday night after the members have gone,' Kyle explained. 'We don't want them seeing the entrance. They might not understand.'

'Not sure I do either,' muttered Christopher as they ascended the steps again. He shivered. Maybe some things were better left to the imagination.

The Waiting Room

It was a wild, dark evening in late
December, and the Dundee train was just pulling
away from the platform as I ran across the
footbridge to try and catch it. I wished I had been
able to talk my sister into driving just a bit faster
on the way to the station, but the wind was
sweeping in from the North Sea and trying to blow
her little car off the coast road, and I could tell she
was nervous.

The train disappeared into the darkness and
I made my way down the rain-slicked steps at a
more reasonable speed. I didn't even know if there
was a waiting-room here. I peered at the signs that
hung above the platform. Yes – there it was. I
could have done with a coffee, but for now getting
out of the elements would have to be enough.

I pushed open the heavy door and took a
step back into the past. Hard wooden seats – an
old-fashioned cylindrical stove in the centre of the
room. Two old people dressed in heavy black
huddled close to it, their hands outstretched to
warm them. They glanced up as I entered. The
man gave a brief nod of greeting, but neither of
them spoke.

'A bit breezy out there,' I remarked, just to
break the silence.

They still didn't speak. Keeping themselves
to themselves. Not everybody enjoyed idle chatter.
I took out my phone and tried to check for

messages, but the signal had gone, and even the battery seemed a bit flaky. It was a pity – I might have used this unforeseen delay to send some messages. I could have checked in with my sister to ask if she got home all right. I could have warned my partner I'd be a bit late home. I wasn't sure exactly how late. I had a vague feeling there were trains on this route about once an hour or so.

There was nothing much to do except watch the old couple and the coal-effect glow coming from the stove. I sniffed the air, which was suspiciously smoky. Was the glow produced by electricity or did the thing actually have coal inside? Wasn't that illegal nowadays? Or at least environmentally unfriendly?

The door opened again and a man in a long overcoat and peaked cap came in, carrying a big old coal-scuttle, which answered my question about the stove. He glanced at me as the others had, but said nothing. It was almost as if there was a pane of glass – or perhaps Perspex - separating me from the others. Even if I had spoken, they might not have heard me. It was an odd feeling.

He went out again, and I suppose about fifteen minutes passed before there was a sound from outside the waiting-room. The old woman nudged the old man, and they gathered their things together and started to leave.

'Wait – is that a Dundee train?' I said, although I hadn't been sure the noise out there had

been made by a train at all. It sounded more like…
But it couldn't be!

They let the door swing closed behind
them, and I had to pull it open again. I emerged
into a cloud of steam that swirled round the
platform and up round the decorative edges of the
canopy above us. The steam should have warned
me. But it just seemed too unlikely to be true.

There was a steam engine standing at the
platform, a line of old-style wooden coaches
behind it. The old couple walked along a little way
and then boarded the train. I began to follow them.

'Tickets, please, sir,' said a voice. I turned to
see the man in the long overcoat, not far away. He
was holding his hand out. I fumbled for my ticket
and gave it to him.

He glanced at it briefly, and then shook my
head at me.

'This is not the train you want, sir.'

'But – does it go to Dundee?'

'Maybe it does. But your ticket isn't valid,
I'm afraid.'

'Never mind that. I'll pay the extra.'

'Oh no you won't, sir,' he said. 'You aren't
on my list.'

'List? What list? I want to travel on this
train.' Even to myself I sounded like a spoilt child.
I added, in case that was what he was thinking too,
'I'm a bit of a steam geek. This is too good a chance
to miss.'

I stepped forward to open one of the carriage doors, but the train was already moving off. I wanted to fling the door open and jump on, but there was a hand on my arm, holding me in place on the platform.

'Let go of me! What are you doing?'

'You can't do this,' said the man's voice again. 'Just calm down. Your train will be along in half an hour.'

I turned to look at him again, planning to expostulate with him, but I got a shock. Since I had last looked, he had swapped his long dark overcoat for a modern jacket with the logo of one of the train companies on it, and had taken off the cap to reveal a head of neatly trimmed fairish hair in an unmistakably modern style. I blinked. He must have been in character for some sort of special event, obviously. But he had certainly contrived to do an almost impossibly quick change.

There was no smell of smoke, no sign of a train vanishing into the darkness. It might as well never have been there.

'Sorry,' I muttered. 'I thought I saw...'

He sighed. 'Yes, we've had this happen here before. It's usually because people have been reading about the disaster and start seeing things. All in their minds, of course.'

'Disaster?'

'You know – the Tay Bridge disaster. A train went over into the river when part of the

121

bridge collapsed. In Victorian times. It was a stormy night like this one. Sometimes people think they see the people, sometimes it's the train.'

'Strange,' I said with an uneasy laugh. Of course I knew about the disaster, but I had never come quite so close to it before.

An hour or so later, crossing the Tay Bridge, I looked down into the river below and gave a shudder. I had seen the remains of the old bridge in the water in daylight of course, but I hadn't really considered what they signified…. A stormy night like this one. What had happened to the old couple from the waiting-room? Did they have to re-live it again and again for as long as there were people like me, who saw things they weren't supposed to see?

That would be the last time I used the waiting-room anyway. It should have some kind of health warning on the door.

The Last Piece of the Puzzle 1

'Nearly finished,' said my mother.

We stared down at the jigsaw puzzle on the table that swung across her bed. We always did them in the same order – first the edge pieces, then the sky, then the sea. All the puzzles had sky and sea in them. She liked landscapes. I wondered whether that had something to do with her diminishing eyesight.

There were ten pieces to go. If you looked at them one way, it seemed there were too many to fit in the spaces that were left, and in another way there weren't enough to fill the gaps. It was only by actually putting them in place that we would find out. The spaces were all in a dark corner of the puzzle, and the only way of anticipating where they might fit was to study the shapes – or by trial and error, which I always felt was giving in.

Phil appeared in the bedroom doorway, mobile phone in hand. 'Time to go.'

'We'd better finish it,' I told him. 'She doesn't like to leave puzzles unfinished.'

'You know the score, Fiona. If we leave it any later, it'll be a nightmare on the motorway, and we won't get home in time for the football.'

'Fifteen minutes max, honestly. Once we've finished this, I still have to do the feeding tube.'

I disliked having to manage the feeding tube, but it was the only way to keep her in her own home. They had given me a lesson on how to do it. I would have been happier if they could have provided a nurse to do it at weekends as well as in the week, but apparently they were short-staffed. We had already been reduced to two carers a day, with the threat of losing one if the funding was cut again. A friend who knew about these things said we were lucky to have any.

Phil disappeared again, and I helped my mother to place a couple more pieces.

'Nearly there,' I said reassuringly, adding two more myself. I frowned. Six to go, and now it definitely didn't look as if there were enough of them. If she had lost one…

I banished that idea from my mind. Only the other weekend we hadn't been able to find a puzzle piece and she had become hysterical, so much so that I had had to stay overnight with her and I'd been on the brink of calling the NHS helpline. Phil had stormed off home and left me to find my way back on the train the next day. Ever since then he had taken to muttering about the parasite generation who should know it was time to make way for younger people.

Three more down, and I knew for sure we must be one piece short.

Phil was in the doorway again. 'You've had ten minutes.'

'There's a piece missing, I know there is.'

He groaned theatrically. 'Not again!'

I helped my mother put in two more pieces. Only one left, and two spaces in the picture.

'She's done this on purpose,' he said, 'just to get you to stay.'

'Don't be silly!' I snapped. 'She's not nearly that devious.'

She fumbled with the last remaining piece, gazing at the puzzle.

'I can't,' she muttered.

'It's all right, Mum,' I said briskly. 'We'll have to put it away now so that I can give you your tea.'

It was ridiculous to call the meals by their usual names when they consisted entirely of liquid gunk, but I harboured the hope that doing so would make things seem a bit more normal.

Her face fell and I was afraid she would start crying again, something that happened at least once during each of our visits. Phil would hate that, of course, but then he hated even coming here, saying he had better things to do. I wasn't sure what they were. He certainly wouldn't have spent his time gardening or doing up the house if we hadn't been here.

I pushed the table aside and took away the puzzle piece she was still holding. This was the worst part of the whole visit. She knew I was just about to leave, and she would resist being fed, although she couldn't keep that up for long.

Phil was hovering in the hall of the bungalow, jingling the car keys, by the time I had finished. I glanced back towards my mother's bedroom and hoped I had done everything properly. I knew I had left her propped up as instructed – she had one of the adjustable beds, operated by a button. Occasionally she had pressed the button herself by mistake, and ended up flat on her back, but I knew she was too weak to do it now, which meant one worry was out of the way.

He held the front door open for me, and he was about to follow me out when he suddenly paused, looking down at the floor in the hall. He swooped and picked something up. He brandished a jigsaw piece at me.

'Here – is this what you were looking for earlier?'

'I suppose so,' I said. 'I'd better put it back in the box – for next time.'

'No, I'll do that,' he said, surprising me with his thoughtfulness. 'She'll only find a way to keep you here. Go ahead, get in the car.'

He tossed me the car keys and I went out to the street and got into the passenger seat. He slid into the driving seat minutes later.

'Was she all right?' I enquired. I always worried that the head of the bed would somehow recline itself again after I had gone. I had been warned of dire consequences if my mother lay completely flat. Still, it shouldn't be long until the carer arrived. She could make any necessary adjustments.

'All quiet on the maternal front,' he said.

I smiled. It was over with for another week.

After we turned off the motorway he said unexpectedly, 'How about we stop off for something to eat? It would save us cooking.'

'That would be nice, for a change. But what about the football?'

'Never mind the football. They'll only lose again anyway.'

We had parked the car and were on our way into the restaurant when my mobile began ringing. He grabbed it from me as I took it out of my pocket and switched it off.

'No interruptions. They can wait until after we've eaten.'

'But what if…?'

'Everybody can wait. Come on, how about some wine?'

'But you're driving.'

'OK, then – wine for you. Coke for me.'

I wasn't used to wine, so it made me pleasantly drowsy, and I forgot all about my mobile until we got home and found the house phone ringing in the empty house. The sound brought me out of my alcoholic haze abruptly, and I rushed to answer it.

The voice on the other end of the line made no sense at first. I had to ask the woman to repeat herself, and even then I didn't really take it in.

'What's the matter, love?' said Phil, walking towards me as I replaced the phone on its stand, taking a few attempts to get it right. 'You look as if you'd seen a ghost.'

'The hospital,' I said, only just managing to get the two words out.

'What?'

'Mum's in hospital.'

'No! But we only left – well, a couple of hours ago.'

'Four hours,' I said, and burst into tears.

It took me a while to explain to him what the woman at the hospital had told me. I didn't know if she had been a nurse or a doctor. Or somebody who had the specific task of breaking bad news to relatives? My mind tried to lead me along that path instead of thinking about the news she had given me. The carer, who had arrived at my mother's house an hour after we had left, had found Mum in some distress, and had called an ambulance immediately. She had been rushed to hospital, but it had proved impossible to save her life.

It was too late. Too late for us to go to the hospital and be with her. Too late to do another jigsaw together.

Somehow I got myself into bed and lay there, wide awake, until I had the faintest glimpse of daylight through the gap in the bedroom curtains. I got up and made a cup of coffee. Phil had managed to go to sleep. But then, he probably didn't have the huge burden of guilt that was weighing me down. In my mind, I went over all I had done before leaving my mother. Was I quite sure the head end of the bed was raised and secured? Had I made some hideous mistake with the feeding tube? Was it in its correct position? Had I given her the right medication?

The doorbell made me jump. I didn't really want to see who was there, but I got up and went into the hall. Through the glass panel in the door I saw two shapes. I frowned. It looked almost as if…

I opened the door. My instinct had been right. There were two uniformed police officers on the step, a man and a woman.

'Mrs Fiona Brown?'

I nodded. They introduced themselves and I invited them in, as they seemed to expect it.

'We're sorry to intrude on you at such a difficult time,' said the woman officer, who seemed to be the senior one, or at least in charge for now. 'Only we understand you visited your mother yesterday, and we have a few questions we need to ask you about your visit.'

Their questions turned out to be rather similar to the questions I'd been asking myself just before they arrived. I ran through the sequence of events for their benefit. In a way it was just as well I'd been through them already, but they did give me a couple of odd looks, maybe because I was able to answer without faltering.

'So you're fairly sure the bed was correctly positioned and there were no problems with the feeding tube when you left?' said the male officer, summing up the story so far.

I nodded. 'Of course there's always the possibility that I made a mistake,' I said, unable to stop myself. 'I'd done it all so many times. It becomes mechanical after a while. I suppose medical staff find the same.'

'Hmm,' said the woman officer.

Then the male one moved in for the kill, like a tiger that had been tracking its prey all along.

'And there was nothing unusual about the medication you gave your mother yesterday?'

'No. It was all set out ready. I'd done it lots of times before.'

The two officers exchanged glances that were probably meaningful to them but which I couldn't interpret.

'If the medication were to be left within her reach, was your mother capable of taking extra doses herself?'

'What? Not really. She was very weak. She couldn't even operate the adjustable bed herself, as far as I know.'

'Mrs Brown, apart from yourself and the carer, was anybody else in a position to give her food or medication over the weekend?'

'No! A nurse comes in on weekdays, but they told us they didn't have the funding for...'

My voice faltered to a stop. What were they saying? Did they have evidence that she had somehow had too much of her medication?

'Is there something wrong?' I asked, after an awkward pause.

The male officer smiled blandly. 'We'll see, Mrs Brown…Were you on your own for that last visit to your mother?'

'No – Phil was with me. I can't drive so he usually takes me there.'

'Your husband?'

'Yes.'

'Thank you for your co-operation, Mrs Brown,' said the woman officer as they got up to leave. 'We may have a few follow-up questions, of course. Is that all right?'

I wondered what they would do if I said it wasn't. Would they leave and never come back?

'What was that about?' said Phil, who had come downstairs as I was showing them out.

I told them what they had said, and the questions they'd asked. He shrugged his shoulders.

'I wouldn't worry – you haven't done anything wrong.'

It was all very well for him to say so. He hadn't even done anything to help me with my mother. He had hardly ever gone near her, and certainly not on his own.

The police came for me again and this time they made it clear they weren't leaving without me. I was standing in the hallway of our house trying to find the words to say goodbye to Phil, twisting my wedding ring round on my finger, when I twisted it once too often and it fell off on to the carpet. He reached down and picked it up for me, and the action brought back a memory.

The jigsaw puzzle piece in the hall! He had taken it through to the bedroom while I went out to the car. So I hadn't really been the last one to see my mother before she was taken ill. I opened my mouth to ask him if she'd been all right when he went in with the puzzle piece, but I closed it again without speaking. I was drained of all energy and all emotion.

As they drove me off in their car I looked back at our house. Phil stood on the doorstep, watching. He had shown no emotion while I was being arrested either.

I couldn't tell them about the jigsaw piece now. They'd think I was making it up to save my own skin. And in a way it was all my fault. My mother. My responsibility. At the very least, I should have protected her, and to make up for my failure I was now protecting him. Would he have done the same for me? It didn't matter much at this point. Without my mother and now without Phil, I had nothing much left.

The Last Piece of the Puzzle 2

'Anything yet, sir?'

'She's a right wee Scheherazade,' muttered the detective inspector, gazing through into the interview room, where the suspect sat still, pale and defiant.

'What?'

'Scheherazade. Telling stories to save her skin. Except that it always comes back to the same story. But what's Mrs Brown afraid of and who is she shielding? She doesn't seem too bothered about her own skin.'

The other officer made a scornful sound. 'You don't have to look very far to answer either of those questions.'

The inspector shook his head. 'She's not about to give up easily. Carries a big weight of responsibility. Says it's all her fault. Her prints are all over everything in her mother's house, of course. Then there are the prints from at least two different carers. Hard to identify the rest. Lot of smudging.'

'He was there too, though, wasn't he? Must have left some trace.'

'Oh, he left prints in the front room and the kitchen all right. And on the puzzle that was on the bedside table... That was odd, though. She said he never helped with the jigsaws. Thought they were a waste of time. She was quite definite on that one.' The inspector sighed. 'Suppose we'd better get on with it. Not that we can do anything much until the lab results come back. There's still an outside chance that it was a natural death. The old woman was on her last legs anyway, by the looks of things. But we still have one of the carers to speak to. And the district nurse, or whatever they call themselves now. The one who did the tube feeding most days.'

'It was a long way for them to come at weekends,' said the other officer, taking another gulp of tea. 'They'd be bound to get fed up with it sooner or later. Start wishing she was dead. Start planning for it.'

'That's a far cry from finishing her off,' said the inspector.

Mrs Brown wasn't saying anything all that new, except that it was rearranged slightly every time they questioned her. If they asked her follow-up questions, she would just burst into tears and say she knew it was all her fault. Otherwise she was quite content to say her piece and then sit there in silence as the time ticked away. Maybe the lawyer had told her the police couldn't do any more until they had some sort of medical evidence to go on. They'd look a bit silly, after all, if they charged her with murder or even manslaughter, and then it turned out the death was natural and even predictable. The doctor had told them either aspiration pneumonia or an accidental or deliberate overdose of the patient's usual medication could have been the cause of death.

But either of these might have occurred without any criminal action, in his view. The lawyer had kept asking for a break in questioning, and certainly his client had every appearance of being on a knife-edge at times. At other times she seemed cool and calm, but only when they weren't asking her anything about the death.

She didn't seem in any hurry to get home. There weren't any children, and she evidently wasn't missing her husband. Another strike against him, in the inspector's opinion. They had heard nothing from the man. He hadn't started nagging at the police to let her go, or to let him see her. There was a man watching the house, and his reports showed that Mr Brown hadn't stirred outside.

'We'll have to get him in for questioning, sir,' said the sergeant who was helping with the interviews. They strolled along the corridor, heading for the canteen.

'I suppose so. But I've got a feeling we should wait for the lab results. He seems like the kind to wriggle out from under us if we move too soon… Can you try and hurry them up?'

'You know what they're like, sir. You'd think they were artists or something. Can't hurry genius.'

He laughed. 'Just give it a try.'

'The carer's coming in after lunch, sir. The one who found the body.'

'Good – maybe we can push things along a bit when she gets here.'

The carer had already given a brief statement to the first officers on the scene, and her account today essentially agreed with that of the doctor.

'She was lying down flat – even I know that isn't good for somebody on a feeding tube,' she told them. 'We always keep the head of the bed up. She was blue in the face, and there was nothing I could do.'

'About the medication,' said the inspector. 'Did you notice anything? Any discrepancy in the amounts already used, that kind of thing.'

The carer frowned. 'I was that shocked, I didn't think to look very carefully. But there was nothing obvious. And it was all marked up by date and time, so if you've brought it here as evidence you'll be able to see for yourselves.'

'They have it over at the lab,' said the inspector. 'Thanks for the tip... Did your visits sometimes coincide with Mr and Mrs Brown's? Or did you just never see them?'

'I did usually see them at lunchtime on Saturdays. They did a bit of shopping, not that there was much of that to do, and tidying up. At least...' She hesitated.

'Please, carry on.'

'She would do all that. I never saw him lift a finger. He didn't even do any of the shopping or help with getting their meal ready. He was just sitting in the front room, doing crossword puzzles.'

'Not jigsaws, then?' said the inspector lightly.

She hesitated again. 'Not usually, no. There was something funny, though. But it probably doesn't matter.'

'Every little helps,' said the inspector, so heartily that the sergeant gave him an odd look.

'Well, it's just that I think he used to sometimes hide the pieces and then Mrs Brown and her Mum couldn't finish the puzzle they were working on. I saw him doing it once, picking one up from the table and shoving it in his pocket when they weren't looking. Then another time I saw him taking a piece out of his pocket and putting it on the table. I don't know if it was even from the right puzzle. It did seem an odd thing to do. Kind of spiteful.'

'I see what you mean,' said the inspector thoughtfully.

After the carer had left, the sergeant said, 'Wasn't there a jigsaw on the table when she was found?'

He nodded. 'Philip Brown's prints were on it, too.'

'Is that enough reason to bring him in?'

'It's a bit tenuous. But it's a possibility...'

He had hardly finished speaking when there was a commotion in the corridor outside. One of the constables burst in.

'She's escaped, sir! Mrs Brown!'

'How the hell did that happen?' said the inspector, heading for the door as fast as he could - not that it would make any difference now.

'She was in the ladies' when the carer went in too, and she got hold of the carer's overall.'

The carer was in the corridor, crying and wringing her hands. 'I'm sorry. I just asked her if she was sure it was really worth it just for him, and she gave me a funny look and grabbed the overall off the top of my bag and made a run for it.'

'You're OK, we'll sort it out later. Don't worry, we'll catch her before she's out of the station. She won't have any money on her so she can't go far even if she gets outside.'

Through renewed sobs, the carer said, 'I had money in my overall pocket.'

'What was that for?' demanded the sergeant. 'Can't you keep it in your purse like everybody else?'

The carer glared at him, still sniffling. 'How was I to know you'd let her escape?'

It turned out that Mrs Brown, wearing the overall, had barged through the security door along with somebody carrying a heap of filing and told them some story about having to rush off to her next client.

The inspector shook his head. 'What did I tell you? Scheherazade!'

'What, sir?' said the sergeant. 'Where do you think she's heading?'

'Anybody's guess. We'll catch her all right, but it's just going to be another big hassle.'

The inspector didn't realise exactly how much of a hassle it would be.

It turned out – of course - that the bus to the town where the Browns lived had just left from a bus stop not far from the police station entrance. An eye-witness told them a wild-eyed woman in an overall had got on it just two minutes earlier.

After a lengthy drive enlivened only by bad language and recriminations, they got out of the car outside the Browns' home. As they advanced up the garden path towards the front door, they heard anguished screams from inside the house.

The two officers looked at each in horror for a moment, but they didn't have any time to waste. The squealing intensified as they advanced towards the door, seeing that it was slightly open just seconds before they tried to kick it in.

'What's he doing to her?' muttered the sergeant.

They came upon a macabre scene in the hallway. A man was huddled in a corner, knees to his chest, arms protecting his head, while the runaway Mrs Brown, still in the carer's overall, hit him about the back and shoulders with a rather small tartan umbrella. He was still conscious, more or less, so she maybe hadn't yet made contact with his head.

She was shouting too – a garbled list of accusations, some of which sounded as if they must date back years.

'...and another thing – you've never even washed a dish or a spoon all the time we've lived together... house would be a pigsty.... the old newspapers.... we might have been out on the streets for all you care... drinking half the night.... and now this! The jigsaw piece...'

'Get her off me!' screeched Philip Brown, peering at the police officers through a gap between his fingers.

'Mrs Brown,' said the sergeant softly. 'You'd be better to put down the umbrella. He'll get what's coming to him, don't you worry.'

The inspector muttered something about not making promises you can't keep. Everybody ignored him.

'Mrs Brown. Give me the umbrella, please,' said the sergeant. 'You're more likely to hurt yourself than him.'

'I don't care!' yelled Mrs Brown. 'I don't care what happens to me. My life's over anyway. My Mum's gone... you'll lock Phil up... There's nothing left!'

'We'll take care of this now,' said the inspector. 'It isn't up to you any longer.'

They heard a sob and then another one, and Mrs Brown turned towards them, the hand that held the umbrella falling by her side as tears streamed down her face.

'He took the jigsaw piece,' she said. 'He pretended he'd found it in the hall when we were leaving her house. He went through to her room to put it back. I wasn't the last one to see her.'

The inspector heaved a sigh. At last! He knew she was telling them the truth this time and not another one of her stories. While the sergeant stepped forward and removed the umbrella from the woman's grasp, he called for backup, keeping an eye on Phil Brown all the time.

'Not tonight, Scheherazade,' he murmured to himself.

Locked Room

It must have been after midnight when I got the call. It was all I needed, after a long shift at the beach, warning off members of the public who should have been safely shut up in their own homes. That wasn't real police work. I had alternately longed for and dreaded a different kind of call, and I had even considered switching off my phone. But this caller was distraught, and I was the only one near enough to respond.

As soon as I opened the door, I realised it was a murder scene. I could see the body right in the middle of the floor, partly covered by a rug. I frowned. What was the point of that? It didn't really conceal anything. Unless the killer had been in the middle of trying to cover it up when he had been interrupted. He or she. Either was possible at this point.

I stepped inside the room, closed the door behind me, and stopped in my tracks when I saw the gleam of eyes in the darkness. Where was the light switch? I fumbled for it and the space was suddenly, starkly lit up, illuminating the scene in all its horror. The body on the floor. The suspects, still close by, gloating over their crime.

There were three of them, sitting in a row and staring at me, their eyes glazed - which was probably because they were all coming down from a high, either because of the killing or from the drugs, or both. I stared back, afraid to look away in case they made a move towards me. One of them was already a killer. I knew the first time was the hardest, and that they might be desperate enough to attack me too now they had the taste for it.

I didn't want to turn my back on them but there were things to be done. I took a few photographs with my phone, just for the record, and recorded some cursory notes. After all, I was first on the scene, apart from the woman who had made the call, of course. I wondered where she had got to.

At last I turned back to the three of them. Their silence was starting to bother me.

'Haven't you got anything to say for yourselves?' I decided I could get away without giving them the official warning in this case. I glared at the largest and ugliest of the gang, who bore the scars of quite a few street brawls, if I was any judge of the matter. 'Not even you? Do you expect me to believe you had nothing to do with this?'

He stared back at me, silent and defiant. I had met villains like him before. They pretended to be hard, but in my experience they were the first to begin sobbing and asking for their mothers if you just faced up to them.

I shrugged, took a piece of chalk from my pocket and began to draw round the outline of the victim. We didn't usually do that these days but I thought it might unnerve them to see me doing it.

But that was my big mistake. I was still bending down with the chalk and wondering if my eyes were telling me the true story about what was on the floor, when one of them jumped me. I squealed with pain as his front claws dug into the back of my neck while the back ones scrabbled up and down my spine for purchase, inflicting damage wherever they touched me. I tried to reach round and wrestle him off me while, out of the corner of my eye, I saw another member of the gang batting at the corpse with her paw until she managed to move it out from under the rug and began chasing it across the kitchen floor.

'What's going on in there?' Somebody rattled the kitchen door. 'Are you OK?'

'Of course I'm not OK!' I screeched. 'Get in here and help.'

'Has it gone?'

'Kind of,' I lied.

'You know I can't help,' she said, sounding almost regretful. 'Why do you think I got you out of bed to deal with it in the first place?'

'Never mind that! Just get in here.'

Of course the ringleader transformed himself into a floppy bundle of fur as soon as she came into the room. She took him from me and glanced round suspiciously. As I straightened up, she pointed over to the corner of the room with the hand that wasn't holding on to the master criminal, and said in a quavering voice, 'It's over there!'

'Just stay where you are – I'll see to it.'

I bravely picked up the thing with my bare hands and took it outside, where I gave it a decent burial under a lilac bush. It was quite a lot of trouble to go to for a catnip mouse, but I couldn't afford to lose any more sleep that night.

About the Author

Cecilia Peartree is the author of the Pitkirtly Mysteries, a 24-book mystery series set in a fictitious small town on the Fife coast. She has also written and published 6 books in the Adventurous Quest series, set in 1950s Britain and beyond, 3 books in the Max Falconer series and a number of historical mysteries with elements of romance (or possibly vice versa). She occasionally writes short stories, examples of which are included above.

Printed in Great Britain
by Amazon

18384078R00088